Unspoken Lies

Unspoken Lies

Darrien Lee

www.urbanbooks.net

Urban Books, LLC
78 East Industry Court
Deer Park, NY 11729

ISBN 13: 978-1-60162-208-2
ISBN 10: 1-60162-208-2

First Printing April 2010
Printed in the United States of America

10 9 8 7 6 5 4 3 2

Distributed by Kensington Publishing Corp.
Submit Wholesale Orders to:
Kensington Publishing Corp.
C/O Penguin Group (USA) Inc.
Attention: Order Processing
405 Murray Hill Parkway
East Rutherford, NJ 07073-2316
Phone: 1-800-526-0275
Fax: 1-800-227-9604

Prologue

Cherise was thankful that no one was at home when the FedEx delivery man arrived on her doorstep. She wasn't expecting a package, but once she saw the return address on the label, her heart sank. She hesitated before opening the letter, and it wasn't until she found the courage to open it and began to read the words that the repercussions of her stormy past became a heart-stopping reality. Her hands trembled as she read line after line. The words seemed to jump off the page, each time hitting her in the gut. It couldn't be true, but it was. Her eyes filled with tears as her sins came back to haunt her with a vengeance. She felt nauseated, and her legs gave out, causing her to sink to the floor.

Her body was numb, and without hesitation, she found the strength to pull her body up from the floor, torch the papers, and toss them into the fireplace. She had to get herself together and fast before her husband, Detective Mason McKenzie returned home with their son, Mason Jr., nicknamed Mase, and her daughter, Janelle. Being a detective, Mason was very perceptive of her moods, and he would know the moment he looked into her eyes that something was wrong. She was a crime scene investigator, and in most cases she was able to subdue her emotions while investigating some of the city's more horrific crimes. When it came to her personal life and her family, things were totally different.

Her family had been through a lot of trials and tribulations over the past year, and things were finally getting back to normal. Now, to have her life shattered by a one-page letter was incomprehensible, and she couldn't let it happen. She could beat this, but she had to stay cool.

The flames radiating from the fireplace warmed Cherise's shivering body as she watched the papers slowly burn down to ashes. If anyone ever found out about the letter, it could destroy everything and everyone she loved. She couldn't let that happen.

Chapter One

It had been three weeks since Cherise received the life-altering letter. So far she'd been able to act normal. On this day, they were sponsoring a cookout/pool party in honor of Janelle and her championship baseball team. Janelle was an all-star on the team, a feat not shared by many young girls her age. Most of them played softball, but it was baseball that fascinated eight-year-old Janelle the most, and her family couldn't be more proud of her.

The aroma of hot dogs and hamburgers radiated in the air as Mason and his brother, Vincent, manned the grills. Fourteen-year-old Mase helped his mother set the tables, while Janelle swam playfully in the pool with her friends. He was very protective and proud of his sister, and often helped her practice in a nearby park. Mase had recently gotten a hardship driver's license due to the unpredictable work schedule of his parents. He'd been driving under the watchful care of his father since he was thirteen, but was unable to make it official until now. He had particular restrictions to follow, but he mostly received it in case of emergencies, or to transport his sister to her ballgames when his parents were unavailable.

Cherise exited the house and made her way over to grill, chatting with parents as she progressed across the lawn. The parents seemed to be enjoying the cold lemonade and iced tea as they listened to music and kept a watchful eye on their children.

"Mason, here's the last of the burgers," Cherise announced as she handed the tray of raw beef to her husband.

"Thanks, baby," he replied. "You can start gathering up the children if you want to. Lunch will be served in five minutes."

She nodded and gave him a subtle kiss on the lips before walking away.

Vincent looked over at Mason and asked, "What's wrong with C. J.?"

Mason looked in her direction and said, "You noticed it too, huh?"

Vincent nodded in agreement.

"I don't know, bro. She's been kind of distracted for a couple of weeks. I asked her if everything was okay and she said it was, but I don't believe her."

"She's pulled a couple of doubles recently, hasn't she? Maybe she's just tired."

Mason flipped the burgers and said, "I don't think that's it. She's used to working doubles. I honestly think it's more than that, but I'm not going to push her. When she feels like talking, she will."

"Do you want me to talk to her?" Vincent asked as he glazed a slab of ribs with his special sauce.

"Nah, leave her alone. She'll eventually come around."

"I hope you're right," Vincent replied. "I'm going to check and see if she needs any help. Do you have anything ready to come off the grill?"

He closed the lid on the grill and then turned to watch the children in the pool. "I will in about three minutes."

"Cool. I'll be back in a second."

Vincent made his way toward the kitchen, stopping to talk to a few parents along the way. He was one of Atlanta's most eligible bachelors, and women of all races and professions found him extremely handsome and irresistible. He could've invited one of the ladies in his life to the cookout, but today it was all about his niece and her accomplishments on the baseball field, and he didn't want any distractions.

Inside the kitchen, Vincent found Cherise spooning baked beans into a large bowl. He walked over to her and asked, "Do you need any help?"

"Actually, I do." She pointed toward the refrigerator and asked, "Can you get the pasta and potato salads out and help me take them out to the table?"

"Sure," he answered as he opened the refrigerator door.

"Thanks for coming over to help."

He turned to her with a huge smile on his face and said, "I wouldn't have missed it for the world. Besides, Janelle would've been awfully angry with me had I not shown up. You know she calls me every day."

She giggled and said, "She loves you very much."

"I love her too," he said as he placed the bowls of salads on a large tray. When he looked up, he noticed Cherise was wiping her eyes.

"Are you crying?"

She wiped her eyes with a napkin and said, "I'm fine. I think I have an eyelash in my eye."

Vincent knew better. In fact, he knew Cherise a lot more intimately than he was proud to admit. He walked over to her, cupped her face, and looked into her eyes, but when he did, he saw sadness.

"I don't see anything in your eye, but I'll blow it anyway."

Then, as gently as possible, he softly blew his warm breath into her eyes. She blinked and wiped a few more tears that had spilled out of her eyes.

"Thanks, Vincent. Whatever it was, it's gone."

He backed away and said, "No problem." But it was a problem because his heart sped up the moment he looked into her eyes. He thought he finally had everything under control, but it was obvious that he still had a long way to go.

"Do you want me to go ahead and take these salads out to the table?"

She smiled and grabbed the tray of hot dogs and hamburgers and said, "Yes. I'm right behind you."

The two walked outside and placed the food on the table. A couple more trips later, all their guests were sitting down to an amazing McKenzie feast of barbecue ribs, chicken, hot dogs, hamburgers, salads, baked beans, and more traditional cookout delicacies. It turned out to be a fabulous season ending celebration.

A few hours later, all that was left to do was bid their guests good-bye, put away the leftovers, clean up, and relax. Cherise and Mason were exhausted, and mellowed out by lounging around the pool, sipping on cool glasses of Chardonnay until Janelle, who was now dressed in dry clothes, abruptly hugged her father's neck.

"Thanks for letting me have the pool party, Daddy."

Mason kissed his beautiful daughter's cheek and said, "You're welcome, baby. I'm glad you had a good time."

Cherise smiled before taking another sip of wine. Janelle crawled into the lounge chair next to her mother and hugged her waist. Cherise ran her hand through her daughter's large curly locks, which were in disarray.

"I love you too, Momma."

She set her wine glass on the table and hugged her daughter. "I know, sweetheart. You're the best daughter a mother could ever ask for."

Janelle smiled with appreciation before sliding out of the

chair. "Are you going to brush my hair before you go to bed?"

Cherise reached up and ran her hand through her daughter's soft locks. "We'll do something with it. Give me thirty minutes and I'll be ready."

Vincent stepped out into the backyard after showering and changing into a pair of dress black slacks, white shirt, and black sports jacket.

"Where are you going all dressed up?" Cherise asked curiously.

Vincent pulled his cell phone off his belt and looked at the screen and laughed without answering.

Mason also laughed and then asked, "What's her name?"

"Don't you worry about it while you're all up in my business."

"Well, wherever you're going, you look nice," Cherise replied. "And don't pay Mason any attention."

"I'm not, and thanks for the compliment," he replied.

Janelle walked over to Vincent and said, "I think you look good too, Uncle Vincent, and thank you for coming to my party."

He knelt down until he was eye level to her, and immediately his heart skipped a beat. He picked her up into his arms and gave her a loving kiss on the cheek.

"I wouldn't have missed it for the world. I'm proud of you. Getting the MVP award two years in a row is a huge accomplishment."

Janelle smiled and then gave her uncle a kiss on the cheek. "I love you, Uncle Vincent."

"I love you too, baby" he replied as he released her and watched as she skipped back into the house.

"She sure is an angel," Vincent pointed out as he pulled his keys out of his pocket.

"That's an understatement," Mason replied as he stood

and patted his younger brother on the shoulders and said, "Come on, I'll walk you out."

Before walking toward the gate leading out into the driveway, Vincent leaned down and gave Cherise a quick peck on the lips. "Good night, C. J."

She held her wine glass up to him and said, "Good-bye, Vincent. Have fun, and thanks again for helping out today."

He winked at her and said, "We're family. That's what we do."

Mason walked Vincent out to his car and chatted with him briefly before returning to the backyard. He pulled Cherise out of her chair and held her quietly in his arms for a moment.

"You smell good."

"You must be drunk," she joked. "I smell like chlorine, smoke, and barbecue sauce."

Mason chuckled before kissing her passionately on the lips. Cherise lay her head against his chest and exhaled. The couple had been through some tough times, and while they loved each other dearly, they were still working on getting their relationship back to where it used to be.

"I guess I'd better go do something with Janelle's curly afro."

Mason released her and picked up the empty wine bottle and glasses and said, "I'm going to take a shower and see if Mase wants to catch a movie."

"I'm sure he'd like that, but what about Janelle?" she asked. "She might wonder why she can't go."

He put his arm around her waist as they walked toward the back door and said, "She'll be fine. I've already talked to her about spending time with them one on one."

"I hope you know what you're doing," she answered, not totally convinced by his confidence. "She is a daddy's girl."

***

Mason was very good with the children when he took the time. His former position as an undercover detective on the Atlanta Police Department's anti-crime unit nearly cost him his marriage, his brother, and his life. Now he was working on rebuilding everything he had torn down, but he knew it was going to be a slow process. His first priority was to repair his broken marriage. Yes, they were still together, and things on the outside looked normal, but it was anything but normal. In fact, their marriage was extremely fragile, and the couple knew they had to proceed slowly if they had any chance of surviving. That's why Mason transferred to the much slower cold case division, which gave him more flexible hours and more time with his family.

Vincent, on the other hand, was one of the city's zone commanders, a lower rank than the chief of police position he'd held in Houston, Texas. He had moved to Houston after suffering from a broken heart, and it took true love and the love for his brother to get him to return to Atlanta. The McKenzie family was on the mend, but only time would tell if their lives would ever get back to normal.

Chapter Two

Vincent pulled up in front of the upscale townhouse in the Buckhead section of Atlanta and shut off his engine. He'd made the date with the thirty-year-old accountant named Elizabeth Fields a few days ago, and now he was having second thoughts. They'd met at the gym recently, and he had to admit that he was attracted to her amazing body and beautiful smile. She was obviously intelligent, athletic, and had a beautiful chocolate complexion. After several short conversations, he'd decided to ask her out. As he sat there, he realized he wasn't very hungry after eating his share of ribs and pasta salad at the cookout. His plan was to take her out to a quaint jazz club for appetizers and drinks, but if she was hungry, he knew he would have to treat her to dinner, and he was fine with that, too.

It was nearly five o'clock, and he couldn't postpone the date any longer, so he climbed out of his black Audi A4 sedan and walked up to the door and rang the bell.

Elizabeth opened the door and greeted Vincent with a warm smile. "Hello, Vincent."

He smiled back at her and said, "Hello, Elizabeth. You look beautiful."

She stepped to the side and thanked him before inviting him inside. Once inside, she saw how his athletic body filled out his dress attire, and it caused her heart to immediately speed up. It has been a while since she'd had a date because she had been concentrating solely on her career. Vincent McKenzie was extremely handsome, and might be more than she could handle. His eyes radiated confidence, and he had no problem looking her in the eyes. He made her feel like he was reading her thoughts, and he if were reading her mind right now, it might reveal all the sinful things she wanted to do with him and that fine body he possessed. She was aware that he was a high-ranking police officer, and she was concerned she might make a fool of herself.

"You have a beautiful home," Vincent complimented her as he took his seat.

"Thank you, Vincent. Can I get you anything to drink?" Elizabeth asked nervously.

She was stunning in an aqua-colored maxi dress with matching sandals, and Vincent immediately picked up on her nervousness. To try to help her relax, he held out his hand and asked her to join him on the sofa. Elizabeth took Vincent's hand and slowly sat down beside him.

Vincent said, "Elizabeth, you're shaking. Are you okay?"

"I will be. Just give me a second," she replied before blowing out a breath.

"Elizabeth, just relax. I'm just the guy from the gym."

"You don't look anything like you do at the gym."

He chuckled and said, "I don't know if I should thank you or be offended."

Embarrassed, she apologized, "Oh, no! I'm sorry. I'm just saying . . . What I meant to say was—"

Vincent kissed the back of her hand and said, "We're just a couple of friends hanging out, Elizabeth. Relax, okay?"

She nodded in agreement after making a fool out of herself.

"Maybe we should get out of here. Are you hungry?"

She stood and picked up her purse and said, "Honestly, Vincent, I think if I eat right now I might throw up."

He opened the door for her and said, "That's a little too much information, but I do have an idea that might make you feel better, if you're up to it."

She turned to him and said, "I'm up for almost anything right now."

As Vincent drove out of the neighborhood, he could sense that she was finally starting to relax. Minutes later, he pulled up at Piedmont Park, a beautiful midtown park with a lake and other amenities. He walked around to the passenger's side of the vehicle and opened the car door.

"Are you up for a walk?"

"I'd like that," she replied before climbing out of the car.

The couple spent nearly an hour and a half in the park getting to know each other. Elizabeth had relaxed even more, and found herself giggling at his jokes as they sat near the gazebo. She found Vincent not only handsome, but humorous as well, and her nervousness had completely disappeared. He had to admit that he was enjoying her company, and for the first time, he felt like he could possibly have a meaningful relationship with a woman like her. The others he'd dated were beautiful with fabulous bodies, but for some reason, they had always had something missing when it came to their personalities. Elizabeth, on the other hand, seemed to have everything together, but he didn't want to speak too soon. Time would tell if things could progress any further.

"Are you ready to grab some dinner?" Vincent asked as he stood and checked the time on his cell phone.

She stood, and with a smile on her face, said, "I'd love to, and before we go any further, I just want to thank you for a lovely evening."

"It's not over yet, Elizabeth," he replied as he naturally took her by the hand and led her back to his car.

Vincent found a quaint, upscale restaurant tucked in downtown Atlanta that had a jazzy ambiance and delicious food. The décor was hip and sophisticated, with various paintings and soft lighting.

Vincent scanned the menu, and while he loved a fine cut of a prime steak, he'd been trying to cut back on his intake of red meat. He decided to get a bacon-wrapped Atlantic salmon with dilled Havarti potatoes and asparagus sautéed in a creamy butter sauce. Elizabeth chose stuffed chicken with lump crab and shrimp, served over a bed of basil mashed potatoes and topped with lemon and caper cream sauce. While they waited for their entrees, they enjoyed the restaurant's signature beignets stuffed with mozzarella and prosciutto, served with basil and jalapeno glaze and a bottle of white wine.

The conversation continued to be enjoyable throughout the rest of the evening, and before the couple realized it, it was nearly eleven P.M. On the drive home, Vincent felt so good that he went ahead and asked her out for the following weekend to a Falcons football game. He explained to her that there was always the possibility that plans could change or get canceled due to his responsibilities as zone commander. Elizabeth assured him that she understood and was looking forward to seeing him again.

Vincent walked Elizabeth to her door and gave her a hug and kiss on the cheek. He thought about pushing things to the next level, but decided against it, even though he felt like she would be a more than willing participant. Instead, he was a gentleman and bid her good night.

***

On the way home, Vincent was called to the unfortunate homicide of a teenage boy outside a twenty-four hour market. It was the second in as many weeks, and it seemed as though an all-out war was brewing among the inner city youth of Atlanta.

When he pulled up to the scene, the area was already roped off with yellow crime scene tape. After showing his badge, he made his way over to his detectives and immediately recognized a familiar physique taking pictures of the victim and crime scene.

"C. J., I didn't expect to see you here."

She lowered the camera and sighed. "Believe me, I'd rather be home than here. How was your date?"

Without making eye contact with her, he leaned down to inspect the young victim.

"It was good."

She studied him for a second and then said, "You like her."

He turned to his sister-in-law and tried his best to suppress a smile. "Now, what are you basing that statement on?"

She continued to take pictures and announced, "I know you, remember?"

"Whatever, C. J.," he replied as he motioned for the detectives on the case to come over.

Cherise smiled and then jotted down some notes in her notebook before giving her assistants some instructions. Vincent discussed the case with his detectives, and before leaving the scene, he instructed them to keep him informed of their progress.

A few hours later, Cherise and her crew had all the pictures and evidence they needed to investigate the case. The medical examiner carted the young man's body off to his lab in order to perform an autopsy.

Vincent met Cherise at her SUV and helped her put the equipment into the back of it.

"Are you heading home?"

"No, I'm going into the office so I can start working on the case."

"It's nearly three A.M. Don't you think you need to start fresh after you've had some sleep?"

She put her hands on her hips and said, "Please! You know that's not how people in our business operate. I want to get the killer of this child off the streets as quickly as you do. If I get tired, I'll take a nap in the office like I always do."

He closed the hatch and walked her around to the driver's side door. Before climbing inside, she looked into his eyes and said, "You're the one who needs to go home and get some sleep. You look exhausted."

"I'm okay."

She touched his face lovingly and said, "You're burning the candle at both ends, brother-in-law."

"I know what I'm doing," he announced convincingly.

"Do you?" she asked. "When are you going to settle down?"

He laughed and then said, "You know where my heart is."

She slid into the seat of her vehicle and said, "Don't go there, Vincent."

Vincent stood in silence outside her vehicle in deep thought. He had fallen in love with her the moment he laid eyes on her, but so did Mason, who at the time was coming off a bad break-up. Vincent wanted to pursue Cherise, but Mason stepped to her before he had a chance, and once he saw how excited Mason was about her, he backed off.

Vincent never had the kind of bad luck with women that Mason had suffered through; he just couldn't find Miss Right until Cherise appeared in their lives. Now, here he was years later, regretting every decision he had made about her and then some. In fact, his love for Cherise hadn't diminished at all; it had increased a million times over and he hated it because she was his brother's wife. While he was happy his brother had found love, he just wished he had found it with someone else, especially since he had mishandled his marriage with Cherise.

"I'm still in love with you, C. J.," he admitted out loud for the first in a very long time.

She sighed and remembered their long passionate affair. He had come to her rescue in some of the darkest times of her life, and she knew without a doubt that she wouldn't have made it without him. He saved her life physically, mentally, and emotionally.

"I love you, too, but not like that. Not anymore."

He reached through the window of her vehicle and caressed her cheek.

"I don't believe you," he replied. "I see it in your eyes, and I hear it in your voice."

Tears formed in her eyes. "I deserve a chance to try and make my marriage work, and you're not making it easy for me."

"I'm sorry about that, but I can't change the way I feel about you."

She started the vehicle and said, "I can't talk about this anymore. I have to go."

Feeling defeated, he stepped back and said, "Drive safely."

Cherise pulled off without responding. Vincent watched as she disappeared down the street and into the darkness. He thought it was going to be easy getting over her, but he was wrong, and now he was unsure if he would ever be able to get her out of his system, or if he wanted to.

The affair began because of Mason's obsession with everything but his wife. He was working undercover on the anti-crime task force, leaving Cherise and his son alone for weeks and sometimes months at a time. When he did come home, he was often distant, evasive, and mysterious. Mason's behavior had become erratic at times, and he pushed Cherise away every time she tried to get close to him. He wasn't the man she fell in love with, and her heart was shattered. Vincent did his best to console Cherise through her pain without crossing the line, but his feelings for her got the best of him, and they ended up in full-blown love affair.

Eventually, guilt and the need for redemption consumed both of them, so Vincent moved to Texas and physically isolated himself from his brother and Cherise for nearly eight years, only keeping in touch via telephone and e-mail, and occasionally visiting during holidays. He thought that distance would get her out of his system, but when he ran into her at a national law enforcement conference, all his feelings came flooding back to him. It was the beginning of what would become a series of dramatic twists and turns in all three of their lives.

Cherise glanced down at her hands on the steering wheel and realized that they were shaking. Vincent has always had that kind of effect on her, even now, and it angered her. She loved Mason and wanted to forgive him, but there was still a lot of pain between them. Recovery for all of them hadn't been easy, but they were family, and family should be able to overcome anything.

As soon as she pulled into the parking garage of her office building, her cell phone rang.

"C. J. McKenzie. How may I help you?"

There was silence on the other end of the telephone.

"C. J. McKenzie," she repeated before looking at the ID, which showed PRIVATE CALL.

Then, before she could speak again, the caller hung up. She tucked the cell phone in her purse and climbed out of her vehicle and made her way toward the elevator so she could get to work. After she stepped onto the elevator and pushed the button for her floor, her cell phone rang again, but this time she looked at the caller ID before answering.

"Hello, Vincent," she answered with a slightly irritated tone.

"Hello, C. J. Listen, I only called to say I'm sorry I upset you. I'll try to keep myself in check around you, but you have to understand that it's hard. I'm going to try a little harder, okay?"

"That means a lot to me."

He paused briefly and then said, "You know how we were together, and it's not something I can just shove under the rug like it never happened. Cut me a little slack, C. J."

She stepped out of the elevator onto her floor and made her way down the hallway to her office. "I don't know if I can do that, Vincent. I mean, I want you in my life, but there has to be some boundaries."

"I understand those boundaries, but not a brick wall."

Cherise set her purse on her desk and sat down. "I owe you, I know that. You were there for me when I was in a lot of pain, and I'll always love you for getting me through that, but we're beyond that now."

"Not emotionally," he replied abruptly.

"Don't you want to see me happy?"

"Of course I do, but you can't dismiss how powerful our love was. You don't get to have that kind of love more than once in your life, so I'm sorry I can't dismiss it as easily as you can."

"I'm not trying to dismiss it or pretend it didn't happen. I'm trying to do the right thing," she explained as she reached over and turned on her laptop. He was right about one thing: their love was powerful, yet forbidden, and it had to be put to rest no matter how she much she cared about him.

"And I commend you for doing the right thing, but you need to cut me some slack. I do have a heart."

"I know you do, Vincent. Look, I have to go. I have another call coming in," she announced. "I'll talk to you soon."

"I understand. Good luck on the case, and call me if you have any problems with my detectives or need any help."

"I will," she replied before clicking over to accept the other call.

"C. J. McKenzie. How may I help you?"

"Hey, babe. I was just checking to make sure you were okay," Mason replied.

"I'm good. I'm in my office getting ready to start working on this case."

"Was it a bad one?" he asked.

"They always are," she answered. "Kiss the kids for me, and I'll come home as soon as I can. Get some sleep, sweetheart."

"I will. I love you."

"I love you too."

Mason turned over in the bed and looked at the clock after hanging up from his wife. It wasn't often that the couple was able to get a full night's sleep, or even sleep in the same bed, because of their work schedules, but it was much better than it used to be. They had made love earlier, and he had hoped to do it again, until she was called out on a case. Now he was wide awake.

After sitting up on the side of the bed, he noticed how peaceful his surroundings were, and then his cell phone buzzed, indicating a text message. He picked it up, expecting it to be a message from his office, but it wasn't even close.

ROSES ARE RED, VIOLETS ARE BLUE. I'M HOT FOR YOU. ARE YOU HORNY TOO?

"What the hell?" he mumbled as he tried to identify the source of the message. He immediately typed a message, inquiring who was sending the message. A few seconds later, he got a response.

THAT'S FOR ME TO KNOW AND YOU TO FIND OUT. SMOOCHES!

Now he was intrigued. Could it be Cherise playing a sexy game with him? Or was it her way of checking to see if he was still being faithful? Just in case, he decided to type one last response.

MY HEART BELONGS TO ONLY ONE WOMAN, AND SHE HAS ALL THE HEAT I NEED.

It was nearly five minutes before he received a reply that nearly knocked him off the side of the bed.

WE'LL SEE ABOUT THAT. GOOD NIGHT, SWEETHEART.

Mason's heart thumped in his chest. As he sat there staring at the message, he wondered if he should send another text. He was more intrigued now than anything. He just hoped it wasn't someone playing a game, because after all the drama he had gone through getting Cherise to trust him again, he wasn't about to let a joke ruin things.

He decided not to reply, in hopes it was just someone playing a joke. He wasn't up for games, so he made his way out into the hallway to check on the kids. He had to admit, he was a little freaked out by the text messages, but remained as calm as possible. He first checked on Mase, who had fallen asleep with his TV on for the millionth time. Mason quietly turned off the TV and made a mental note to remind him once again to set the sleep timer before going to bed.

He entered Janelle's room and immediately stubbed his toe on what felt like a baseball helmet. It was in the middle of the floor, even though he had told her time and time again to put away all of her equipment and clean her room before going to bed. He wanted to yell, but he knew if he did, he could possibly scare her, and that was the last thing he wanted to do. She was his angel, and she meant the world to him, so after he tenderly kissed her forehead, he eased out of her room and back to his own.

Not able to sleep, he decided to go downstairs to grab a cup of coffee and a bagel before working out on the elliptical machine. He had a mystery on his hands, and a good workout was just what he needed to get his mind working to solve it one way or the other.

Chapter Three

It had been more than twelve hours since Cherise was called out on the homicide. Mason and the children had attended church, and were now having dinner with Cherise's parents, Jonathan and Patricia Jernigan. This was a ritual they followed at least once a month, Vincent included. On this day, like most Sundays, Patricia had outdone herself in the kitchen. There was pork roast, scalloped potatoes, turnip greens, cornbread, garden salad, and peach cobbler. She prepared her famous fruit tea and lemonade for the children.

As the children helped Patricia set the table, Jonathan showed Mason their brand new gold Cadillac CTS in the driveway. He'd always been a Cadillac man, and both he and Patricia had worked hard all their lives as physicians, so they could retire comfortably. Jonathan and Patricia were in their sixties, but they didn't look a day over fifty. They'd been married for forty-five years and showed no signs of slowing down. Most days you could find them either out on the lake in their three-bedroom houseboat, on the golf course, or spoiling their grandchildren.

As they stood out in the driveway talking, Vincent pulled up and exited the vehicle with a bag in his hand.

After shaking hands, Jonathan asked, "What's in the bag?"

"Ice cream and whipped cream," he revealed. "Patricia called and asked if I could pick it up for her peach cobbler."

All three walked into the house together, and while Vincent put the items in the refrigerator, Mason eased out onto the deck to call Cherise.

"Hello?"

"Hey, babe, I know you're probably exhausted, but I was checking to see if you were going to make it over to your parents' for dinner."

"I'm on the way. I should be there in about fifteen minutes."

"Okay, drive safely."

Mason hung up the telephone, and before he could walk into the house, he received a text message, stopping him.

ROSES ARE RED, VIOLETS ARE BLUE, ENJOY YOUR SUNDAY DINNER UNTIL I CAN ENJOY YOU.

More and more he was beginning to believe Cherise was sending the messages. Each time, they started after he'd spoken with her, but to be on the safe side, he'd tread lightly. This time he wouldn't respond. Instead, he would wait until Cherise arrived to see if she gave away the fact that she was the culprit behind the mysterious texts. He rejoined the rest of the family and took his seat.

"Cherise is on the way," he announced. "She'll be here in fifteen minutes."

Vincent nodded as he picked up a carrot to snack on. Patricia had put out a fruit and vegetable tray for everyone to nibble on until dinner was served. Janelle watched Vincent eat the carrot, so she picked one up and dipped it in the Ranch dressing before taking a bite.

"It's good, isn't it?" he asked her.

She put her arm around his neck and said, "I love carrots, Uncle Vincent."

"That's why your eyes are so pretty."

"Thank you, Uncle Vincent. They're just like my mom's."

He kissed Janelle on the cheek and said, "They sure are, sweetheart."

Janelle giggled and continued to snack on the fruit and vegetables.

A few blocks away, Cherise made her way down the four lane road near her parents neighborhood. She hated being late to anything, especially to family dinners. Just then, a dark four-door sedan cut her off, causing her to swerve her vehicle into oncoming traffic. Horns blared and she nearly lost control of her truck. Cherise struggled as she barely missed a head on collision with a dump truck. Her heart was pounding in her chest as she eventually regained control of the vehicle and came to a stop in a nearby parking lot. When she looked up, the dark sedan was long gone. After calming herself, she said a short prayer and continued the short drive.

"Sorry I'm late," Cherise apologized as she entered the house.

Mason greeted her with a kiss and said, "Actually, your timing is perfect. We were just snacking until you got here."

Janelle hugged her mother's waist and said, "I missed you, Momma."

"I missed you too," she replied as she leaned down and kissed her daughter.

Patricia walked into the family room and cupped her daughter's face. After kissing her on the cheek, she said, "Hey, sweetheart."

"Hi, Momma."

Patricia frowned and asked, "What's wrong?"

Cherise stepped out of her mother's embrace. She walked

over to the table and picked up a cucumber to eat. "Nothing's wrong, Momma."

Patricia put her hands on her hips and said, "I know when something is wrong. You can't fool me."

Mason looked over at Cherise and asked, "Is everything okay, babe?"

This also got Vincent's attention. He studied her body language. He knew that when she fidgeted, something was up.

"I said I was fine," she reiterated as she nodded toward the children. The last thing she wanted was for them to think something was going on.

Jonathan interrupted everyone and said, "She said she was fine, so drop it, Patricia. I'm hungry. Let's eat."

Cherise put her hands up and said, "Before we leave the room, I want to remind everyone about Mason's birthday next weekend. The invitations have gone out, the caterer and DJ both have been booked, but I might need your help decorating."

Janelle clapped with excitement, while Mason appeared to blush.

"Sweetheart, you don't have to do all of this for my birthday. As long as I have you and my family, that's all the celebrating I need," he announced.

Vincent threw a carrot at his brother and said, "No sense whining now because it's a done deal. Let your wife do her thang, bro. It'll be the perfect time for you guys to meet Elizabeth."

Mason threw the carrot back at Vincent and asked, "Is that the girl you've been dating?"

"Yes, that's her. I think you'll like her."

Jonathan clapped his hands together and said, "I'm sure we will, Vincent. Cherise, let us know what you need for the party. We'll assist you in any way possible. Now, are we going to eat or not?"

"Just a second, Daddy. You'll get to eat in a second. This is important," she announced. "Mason, I know you don't like a lot of attention, but you deserve this party."

"Whatever you want, baby," he replied.

She smiled and said, "Great! I want to do something with just the family on your birthday, so make sure you work it out with your job so you can be off."

He gave her another kiss on the lips. "Thank you, sweetheart. A grown folks' party with some dancing sounds great. I can show everyone my moves."

"Your moves?" Vincent asked. "The last time I saw you dance it looked like you had two left feet."

Everyone laughed as they finally made their way into the dining room for dinner. They all held hands so Jonathan could bless the food. The family quickly filled their plates and dug into a smorgasbord of delicious food and drinks.

A few times during dinner, Patricia noticed Cherise yawning. She understood the kind of hours she worked, and she also understood the toll it took on a person's body, especially a woman. Maybe that was what had her out of sorts.

"Cherise, why don't you go upstairs and lay down for a while? I'll pack up some food for you to take home so you can eat later."

She waved her mother off and said, "You don't have to do that. I'll rest once I get home."

Mason put his arm around her shoulders and massaged her neck.

"Well, you're not driving home. I don't want you falling

asleep at the wheel. Jonathan or Vincent can drive your car home, while you ride with me."

She smiled, laid her head on his shoulder, and replied, "I'd like that."

Cherise yawned again, causing everyone to laugh. She didn't want to put a damper on Sunday, so she took her mother up on her offer and excused herself from the table. "I think I'll go upstairs and take that nap after all."

Jonathan took a sip of tea and said, "Sleep as long as you like. We're going to be watching the football game for a while."

Cherise hugged her father's neck and then kissed him on the cheek. "Thank you, Daddy."

Vincent wiped his mouth and said, "I'm going to have to take a rain check on the game and driving C. J.'s car home. I have a date."

"Don't worry about it, Vincent. I can drive her car home," Jonathan answered.

Hearing the news about Vincent's date caught Cherise's attention. This was the second time she'd come up today, and Vincent hardly ever mentioned his dates during family time. Wanting to hear more, she decided to remove empty dishes from the table and take them into the kitchen so her interest in the subject wouldn't be so obvious.

Patricia playfully smacked Vincent on the hand and said, "You come to my house to eat up my food, then you go see some young thang for dessert. My heart is wounded, Vincent."

Patricia and Vincent often joked innocently with each other over dinner.

"I'm with Patricia on this one, bro. You're dissing the family on Sunday?" Mason asked.

Vincent laughed and then said, "Yeah. She's a beautiful woman."

28 Darrien Lee

"This is the second time you've gone out with her, right?" Mason asked.

He glanced over at Cherise standing in the kitchen and saw a glimpse of jealousy in her eyes. "Officially, yes. We see each other at the gym, so we've hung out there a few times."

"I bet she's fine since she spends a lot of time at the gym. What does she do?" Mason asked as Cherise walked back into the dining room to remove more dishes before she headed for the stairs.

As she climbed the stairs, she could still hear the conversation going on in the dining room. Vincent continued to fill the family in on his new love interest.

"She's an accountant," Vincent revealed. "And your suspicions are correct. She's very fit and has curves out of this world."

"She's intelligent, fine, and beautiful. Sounds like a winner to me," Mason replied.

"Well, if you ask me, you've been single long enough," Patricia announced. "It's time you settle down and start your family. Maybe she'll be the one."

Vincent kissed Patricia's hand and said, "I don't know about all that. I just started dating the woman. Don't put me at the altar too quickly."

"What's wrong with that, son?" Jonathan asked. "You're going to need a good woman to grow old with. I have Patricia, and Mason has Cherise. There's nothing like having a good woman by your side."

"I can't argue with you on that. Patricia, as usual, dinner was off the chain, but I have to get going."

"You're always welcome, Vincent, and thanks for bringing the ice cream."

"It was my pleasure," he replied as he stood and pushed his

chair up to the table. "I'm going to tell C. J. good-bye before I leave. Kids, I'll see you later."

"Okay, Unc," Mase replied.

"Mason, I'll holler at you later," Vincent announced as he gave him a brotherly hug. "Jonathan, it's always a pleasure."

Jonathan pointed at Vincent and said, "Likewise, and I want to see you on the golf course soon if you can work me into your schedule."

"Without a doubt," Vincent answered as he shook Jonathan's hand and headed toward the stairs.

"Aren't you going to tell me good-bye, Uncle Vincent?" Janelle asked as she stared at him with her hands on her hips.

"Of course I am, Janelle, but let me go up and tell your mother good-bye first before she falls asleep."

Upstairs, Cherise removed her shoes just as a soft knock on the door got her attention.

"Come in," she called out softly.

Vincent walked in and smiled. "I didn't mean to disturb you. I just wanted to tell you good-bye before I leave."

"That was thoughtful," she replied as she stood and walked over to the dresser to remove her earrings.

He couldn't help but admire her fabulous body as she walked across the room. Just being in close proximity to her was causing his body to defy him, so he decided to make a quick exit.

"Are you okay?" he asked curiously.

She turned to him, and with an irritated tone, said, "For the millionth time, I'm fine."

He shoved his hands in his pockets and chuckled. "You're lying. I know you, remember?"

They stared at each other for a second, until she broke the silence. "I know you know me, but that doesn't mean I'm hiding something."

Vincent smiled and rubbed his chin and then said, "You usually look me in the eyes when you talk to me, and for some reason, you can't seem to do it today. That's making me think that you're hiding something."

She casually walked over to him and stood within inches of him. "Is this better?" she asked as she stared up into his eyes.

His lower region was aching now, and he did the only thing he could possibly do to keep from ruining their relationship. He kissed her forehead and said, "Good-bye, C. J."

"Good-bye. Drive carefully."

He stepped out into the hallway and said, "Will do."

Outside, Vincent looked up at Cherise's bedroom window. Now he had to get his head focused back on his date with Elizabeth. She was definitely a beautiful woman who would probably make the average man very happy, but there was only one woman who had ever been able to handle him mentally, emotionally, or physically—and she was unavailable.

When Vincent pulled up at Elizabeth's house, she was anxiously waiting.

"Hello, Vincent." She greeted him with a warm hug.

"Elizabeth, you look stunning."

Elizabeth blushed. She was wearing a pair of designer jeans with a decorative red-and-black silk blouse in the Atlanta Falcons team colors, and a pair of black stiletto sandals.

Vincent wanted Elizabeth to choose the location for their outing today since he picked it last time.

"So, where do you want to go?" he asked as they climbed into his car.

"How about the ESPN Zone?"

He smiled and said, "Elizabeth, you don't have to go somewhere on my behalf. Pick anywhere."

She reached for her seatbelt and said, "I did, and I picked

the ESPN Zone. I like football, and I don't want to miss the game."

He laughed and said, "Okay. You're the boss."

Vincent was impressed and happy that Elizabeth loved football. He'd dated women who didn't know the difference between football and baseball, and while it wasn't a requirement in the relationship, it did make for some great days to the Georgia Dome and Turner Field.

At the ESPN Zone, the couple was escorted to a table facing the giant TV screens. The waitress handed them menus and then left to get their beverages.

"So, Vincent McKenzie, what do you have a taste for?"

He closed his menu and said, "Well, I have to admit that I'm not very hungry. I have a standing dinner engagement with my family one Sunday each month, and I may have overdone it a bit."

"That's sweet. There's nothing like spending time with the ones you love."

"I agree," he replied as the waitress returned to the table with their drinks.

Elizabeth thanked the waitress for their drinks. After the waitress walked away with their order, Elizabeth took a sip of her Corona and said, "Listen, Vincent, if you want to cancel dinner and go out another day, it's okay with me. The last thing I want to do is interrupt family time."

Vincent looked over at Elizabeth and took her hand into his. "That's not necessary, but it's nice of you to offer. Besides, I wanted to see you."

She gave his hand a soft squeeze and said, "I wanted to see you too."

As they sat there holding each other's hands, a silence fell over the couple. Sensing the awkwardness, Vincent released her hand and took a sip of his raspberry tea.

"Speaking of my family, my sister-in-law is giving my brother a birthday party next weekend, and I would like you to meet them."

Elizabeth's eyes lit up, and with a smile, she said, "I'd like that. Make sure you let me know what attire is. I'd hate to show up casual if everyone else is going to be dressed up."

He crunched down on ice and said, "Just dress like you're going out dancing, because that's what we're going to be doing anyway."

"I can't wait," she said. Thanks for inviting me."

He winked at her and said, "It's my pleasure."

Elizabeth tried not to grin too hard. She bit down on her lower lip and then asked, "So, am I the only one who's going to have a beer?"

"It does look tasty, but I can't drink since I'm your chauffeur for the evening."

She took another sip and said, "I'm so glad you take that seriously. A lot of people don't think and end up ruining their lives."

Vincent nodded in silence as he looked up at the TV screen at the pre-game commentary.

"Then again, ribs are not ribs unless you have a cold beer."

He glanced over at her and said, "That's cold, Elizabeth."

"I'm just teasing you, Vincent. I appreciate the fact that you take my safety and yours seriously."

"I'm a police officer. It's my duty," he replied.

"Tell me about your family. How many brothers and sisters do you have?" Elizabeth asked before taking another sip of her Corona.

Vincent's eyes lit up as he began to talk about the family. "It's only me and my brother, Mason. No sisters. Mason's a detective in the cold case division. He's married to Cherise, who's a crime scene investigator, and they have two children: Mason Jr., who's fourteen, and Janelle, who's eight. Cherise's mother, Patricia, enjoys cooking, so she always hosts dinner one Sunday each month with her husband, Jonathan. A lot of times, we can't because of our careers."

"They all sound wonderful," she replied. "I can't wait to meet them."

"Me too," he answered.

"So, Vincent McKenzie, how is it that you're not married yet?"

He laughed and said, "I could ask you the same thing."

"Touché," Elizabeth answered as she held her glass of beer up to him. "I guess I deserved that. Seriously, Vincent, why aren't you married? You're obviously handsome, fit, and from what I've been able to see, you're a perfect gentleman. What's up?"

"It's simple. I haven't found the right woman yet."

"You're not looking for Miss Perfect, are you?" Elizabeth asked curiously as the waitress returned with their appetizers, which consisted of a tray of hot wings, baby back ribs, spinach dip, bite size cheeseburgers, and chicken tenders.

Once the waitress had left their table, Vincent was finally able to answer her question.

"I'm not looking for Miss Perfect, but I do believe that it's going to take a unique woman to fit into my lifestyle. Police officers don't have regular schedules. We're away from home a lot, and then there are ups and downs emotionally because of the types of cases we have to work. I'm going to need a wife who can deal with all that and then some."

Elizabeth thought about Vincent's description of his future wife and agreed that it would take a special woman to be his wife. Whether she could actually fill the job was questionable, but she was definitely intrigued about the possibilities.

"Now it's your turn. Why aren't you married?" Vincent asked Elizabeth.

She cleared her throat and then said, "Well, I came close once, but I caught him cheating, so I kicked him to the curb."

"Sorry to hear that," Vincent replied. "Unfortunately, there are still a lot of assholes out there that don't know how to treat women."

"All he had to do was be honest with me. If he didn't want to get married, he should've said something."

"Sadly, some men want to have their cake and eat it too," Vincent said. "You should be thankful you saw his true colors before you married him."

"I am thankful, but it still hurt. I guess that experience made me a little gun shy of pursuing another relationship."

"So you just threw in the towel?" Vincent asked.

"Vincent, I can't handle that kind of pain again. My heart was broken and my trust was violated. Can you blame me?" she asked.

"No, I don't blame you, but love is not something you can easily dismiss. I know that for a fact."

Vincent's comment intrigued Elizabeth, and even though they had only known each other for a short time, she was curious about him.

"So, you've been in love before?" she asked.

"Yes, I have," he replied as he looked back up at the TV screen. Vincent's thoughts immediately went back to Cherise, and his instincts were telling him that their conversation was about to go a lot further than he wanted it to. Revealing any more of his personal life wasn't on the menu for today, and now was the perfect time to change the subject. Luckily, he didn't have to, because the room erupted in cheers once the team kicked off.

Chapter Four

Hours later, Cherise woke up from a long nap and sat up on the side of the bed. On the pillow next to her was a note from Mason.

Sweetheart,

I hope you got some rest. I got called in on one of my cases. I should be home by midnight.

I love you,

Mason

Cherise slid the note down in her purse and made her way into the bathroom to freshen up. Before heading downstairs, she turned on her cell phone and noticed that she had a message. She prayed it wasn't her office calling her back into work, but if it was, she would have to go, especially if there was some updated information on one of her cases. As she stood in front of the mirror, brushing her hair, she listened to the message. As expected, it was work, but they only wanted to update her on one of her cases. After hanging up, her mind went back to the driver who cut her off and how close she came to crashing. The kids could've easily been in the car with her. Now she was anxious to get home and out of harm's way.

When she appeared in the family room, Janelle called out to her as she jumped up and hugged her waist.

"Momma, you've been 'sleep for a long time."

"I know, baby. Get your jacket so we can go home. You have school in the morning."

Jonathan turned the volume down slightly on the TV and said, "Why don't you guys just spend the night? You all have clothes here, so there's no need to leave."

"I know, but I'd rather get the kids home. I haven't been home in over twenty-four hours, and I just want to sleep in my own bed."

He stood and kissed her forehead. "I understand, honey. Are you rested enough to drive? If not, I can take you, and your mother can pick me up."

"Thanks, Daddy, but I got it. Where is Momma?" she asked as she looked at her watch.

"She took a plate next door to Mrs. Livingston. She's still recovering from her hip surgery."

Cherise gave her father a kiss and said, "Oh, Daddy, I'm sorry to hear that. Give Mrs. Livingston my regards, and let Momma know I'll call her tomorrow. Come on, kids, we have to go."

Jonathan put his arm around his daughter's shoulders as he walked her to the door. "I will, sweetheart. Drive safely. I love you, Cherise."

Cherise kissed her father's cheek and said, "I love you too, Daddy. Thanks for dinner and everything."

"Anytime, sweetheart."

Hours later, Cherise sat out on the patio near the outdoor fireplace and thought about the last twenty-four hours. Between her job and the near fatal car crash, she was a little stressed. It was a chilly evening, and the only things that calmed her was the warmth of the fire, the Chardonnay she was drinking, and her nine millimeter sitting in her lap. She never liked sitting outside at night unarmed when Mason wasn't home. She peeped down at her watch and hoped he would be home by midnight, like he promised. While he still worked long hours, it was nothing compared to the dark days of his undercover stint.

Just then, her cell phone rang, startling her. When she looked at the caller ID, it showed OUT OF AREA on the screen, so she let it go into her voice mail. The symbol alerting her to a message popped up on the screen, and then three seconds later, the cell phone immediately rang again, but this time it showed PRIVATE. She pushed the button, sending it into voice mail once again, and then she turned her cell phone completely off. She was determined to try to get a good night's sleep, so after dousing the fire with a pitcher of water, she made her way into the house and up to bed. Then, just as she was about to turn off the light, the home phone rang.

"Hey, babe. Did I wake you?" Mason asked.

Cherise let out a breath and said, "No, but I was just getting ready to turn in. I wish you were here. It's been a tough twenty-four hours."

"I'm sorry," he apologized. "I'll be home as soon as I can. I just wanted to check on you and the kids before it got any later. I love you."

"I love you too. Be careful," she reminded him before hanging up the telephone.

The next afternoon, Vincent walked into the CSI office dressed in his commander's uniform, and his broad shoulders filled it out with perfection. The receptionist and all the other female employees on the floor seemed to fall apart whenever he was around, because his sex appeal was so powerful. He'd known most of them for several years, and even casually dated a few of them.

"Good afternoon, Commander McKenzie," the receptionist greeted him.

Vincent leaned against her desk and said, "Hello, Keira. You're looking lovely as ever today."

She fluffed her hair and then blushed. "Thank you, Commander."

Even though Keira was happily married, she always appreciated a fine man in uniform.

"You're very welcome," he replied. "Is C. J. in her office?"

She looked down at her telephone and said, "Yes, but she's on the telephone right now."

"Is it okay if I go in?"

Keira smiled and said, "I'm sure she won't mind. Just poke your head in and she'll let you know if it's okay to come in. It's nice seeing you again, Commander."

"It's always nice to see you too, Keira," he replied before waving at all the other pairs of female eyes that were staring at him before he walked away.

Vincent made his way down the hallway to Cherise's office and slowly opened the door. She looked up at him and momentarily stuttered on the telephone. After waving him into the office, she ended her call and greeted him with a smile.

"Hello, Vincent. What brings you down here?"

He sat down in the chair across from her and crossed his legs and asked, "Why haven't you returned my phone calls? I called you a couple of times last night and I sent you an e-mail this morning."

"Can't you at least say hello before biting my head off?" she asked, getting up from her desk and walking over to a bookshelf.

"Hello, C. J. Now, tell me why you been playing me off."

"I've been busy," she replied as she searched for a particular book on the bookshelf. "I was going to call you when I got a moment."

She was purposely avoiding eye contact with him for some reason, and he couldn't help but be intrigued.

Cherise glanced at him from across the room and said, "You know how busy it gets down here. Besides, all you said on your messages was to give you a call. If it had been something urgent, I'm sure you would've said so."

He didn't believe her, but for now, he'd let it go. Cherise found the book she was looking for, and when she approached her desk, she realized he had been staring at her.

"Stop staring at me, Vincent."

He chuckled and then unbuttoned his jacket. "I'm sorry. I didn't realize I was staring."

"Well, you were, so stop. You know it makes me uncomfortable."

"You're beautiful, C. J. You don't make it easy for a brotha."

With a smirk on her face, she opened her mouth to speak, but he interrupted her.

"Listen, I didn't come down here to pick a fight with you. I only called last night to tell you that Elizabeth was coming to Mason's party with me and that if you need any help with the party, let me know."

Cherise looked up at him and said sarcastically, "You don't have to approve your dates with me."

He laughed. "I'm not asking for your approval. I'm just telling you because I want you guys to meet her."

Cherise stopped typing on her laptop for a moment and looked into his handsome brown eyes.

"I'm sorry for acting so bitchy today. It's been kind of crazy around here, and I've been working on this case."

Vincent interrupted her and said, "Apology accepted."

"Thank you," she whispered. "Listen, I want to thank you

for helping me with the party too. I'm going to need you to put up some lights and a few other things. The caterers are handling everything else."

"No problem. What about the cake? Do you need me to pick it up?"

"Yes, if you don't mind, but please be careful with it. I had it made in the image of a fifty-seven Chevy convertible. You know Mason loves those classic cars."

"Yeah, I know. Don't worry," he assured her. "I'll be extra careful."

The two of them sat in silence for a few seconds. The attraction to her was strong, but he decided not to let his emotions get the best of him. Instead, he decided to take their conversation in a different direction.

"So, what did you get Mason for his birthday?" he asked.

Cherise jumped out of her chair with excitement, walked around to the front of her desk, and leaned against it. Vincent instinctively glanced down at her shapely legs and shook his head. He had a long memory, and seeing her thighs in that short skirt was intoxicating. It was taking every fiber in his body to keep from saying or doing something he'd later have to apologize for.

"Vincent!" she yelled as she stood and folded her arms. "Are you even listening to me?"

He was busted, but honestly, he didn't care because he always had a huge admiration for her body.

"I'm sorry, but you have me a little distracted," he admitted.

She stared down at him and softly replied, "Here I am trying to tell you about my husband's gift, and your mind is a million miles away."

"My mind wasn't a million miles away; it was right here in this room with you."

Frustrated, Cherise put her hands up to him in defense. "I can't keep doing this with you."

He stood, looked into her beautiful brown eyes, and kissed her on the corner of her lips. "Then stop fighting it."

"There's nothing to fight!" she yelled at him.

Vincent frowned and said, "Whatever, C. J. I'm out. Give me a call or shoot me an e-mail and let me know where I need to pick up the cake, and anything else you need me to do."

Cherise followed him over to the door and put her hand on top of his, preventing him from opening it. "Wait! I don't want you to leave angry."

"I'm not angry," he revealed. "I respect your decision."

She held his hands and said, "Seriously, because this is hard for me too."

"You could've fooled me."

Cherise caressed Vincent's arm and said, "Vincent, I have comfort in knowing that we're always going to be connected to each other, no matter what."

A few tears rolled down her cheeks unexpectedly. He reached over and wiped them away before she had a chance to.

"It's okay," he softly replied. "I didn't come here to stress you out."

She hugged his neck and said, "I know, and I love you for that."

He opened the door and smiled. "I love you too. Now, get back to work. I'll holler at you later."

She nodded and watched as he walked out of her office, closing the door behind him. It was hard for her to ignore his strong feelings for her and she had to admit she wasn't one hundred percent over him, but she was making a strong effort to commit herself to Mason and their marriage. It was, after all, a miracle they were still alive. If it hadn't been for Vincent risking his life, shielding her and Mason from a crazed gunman, they would be dead. It was a close call, and Vincent almost lost his life in doing so. Now they were trying to heal, not only physically, but emotionally. The trio had a long way to go, and the most delicate relationship out of all of them was the one between the two brothers. Mason had forgiven his brother for the affair after he saved their lives, and he prayed each and every day that Cherise had forgiven him for his countless infidelities. The relationship was fragile, but well on the road to recovery.

Later that evening, Mase and Janelle arrived home after school, where they were met by Mason, who was just about to put dinner on the table. Janelle greeted him with a big hug and kiss before running down the hallway.

"Hey, guys, wash your hands so you can eat!" he yelled out to them. "I have to go back to work. Your mother should be home a little later."

Mase opened the refrigerator and pulled out a Pepsi, but before he could open it, Mason took it out of his hand.

"No soda before dinner, son. Go wash your hands so you can eat. You can get a Pepsi after dinner. I want you and Janelle drinking more water and milk."

He let out a frustrated sigh before picking up his book bag and heading toward the stairs. Moments later, Mason sat down and enjoyed his signature meatloaf, mashed potatoes, and peas with his children. While at the dinner table, he received an unexpected text. He hadn't received one in a while, and he had hoped the pranks were over.

HEY, BABY! I'VE MISSED YOU. I CAN'T WAIT TO FEEL THAT FINE BODY OF YOURS AGAINST MINE. KISS! KISS!

Janelle was in the middle of telling a story about something that happened to her at school, but Mason was distracted by the text.

"Daddy!" she yelled.

Startled, he set the phone down on the table and said, "I'm sorry, sweetheart. What did you say?"

Mase, being the teenager he was, said, "I thought you said no texting at the table, Dad."

"I know what I said, and I don't need you to remind me. You know I get texts from work, but if I didn't set those rules, you and Janelle would sit here and text throughout dinner," he explained before he stood and removed the empty plates. "You two hurry up and finish so you can clean up the kitchen. I have to leave shortly."

Janelle followed her father into the kitchen and said, "Daddy, are you going to let me finish my story?"

"Of course, sweetheart. Grab those other plates and come into the kitchen with me. I'd love to hear your story."

Janelle hurried back into the dining room and gathered the plates as she was told, so she could tell her father her story for the second time.

After making sure the kids were settled, Mason made his way out the door and back to work. It wasn't until nearly an hour later that Mase discovered that his father had left his cell phone on the dining room table. He expected him to come home any minute to retrieve it, but until then, Mase would have a little fun with the tricked-out cell phone. It had a lot of fancy games on it, so Mase took it into the family room and started playing some of them until a text message popped up, interrupting him.

HEY, BABY, I HOPE YOU'VE MISSED ME AS MUCH AS I'VE MISSED YOU. I CAN'T WAIT TO SEE YOU.

"What?" Mase mumbled to himself, and even though he knew he was wrong for reading his father's text messages, he decided to scan through the other messages as well. One erotic message after another popped up on the screen as he continued to scan through them. He saw the ones his father had exchanged with his mother, but the more seductive messages had the number blocked. What surprised him even more was that his father had responded to some of them.

Angry, Mase jumped up off the sofa and put the telephone back in the dining room where he'd found it. Forty-five minutes later, he heard his father return home. The young teen didn't want to believe that his father was cheating on his mother, but unbeknownst to his parents, he knew of some of their past marital troubles. He'd seen his mother crying on more than one occasion. He didn't want to believe his father was being unfaithful to his mother once again.

Chapter Five

Vincent tossed his keys in the glass bowl as he entered his home. As he removed his tie and unbuttoned his jacket, the conversation with Cherise was still fresh on his mind, and he would swear he could still smell her perfume. They had a passionate history together, and he'd tried his best to back off, but it hadn't been easy. It was obvious she was desperately trying to repair her marriage, and it seemed like they were finally getting things back on track. Unfortunately, Vincent knew a lot more about Mason's past infidelities than she did, but it wasn't up to him to reveal anything to her. If she knew more details, it might hinder their reconciliation and end their marriage once and for all.

After removing his shirt, Vincent was making his way across the floor of the spacious loft toward his bedroom when his cell phone rang.

"Hello?"

"Hello, Vincent. Is this a good time?" Elizabeth asked.

He smiled and took a seat at the island kitchen table. "Yes, it's a good time. How was your day?"

"Long and stressful," she replied as she wiped her tired eyes. "What about yours?"

"It was about the same, and I swear if I have to go to one more meeting today, I might pull out my gun and shoot myself in the foot."

Elizabeth giggled. "You don't mean that. Are you still at work?"

"No, I actually just got home and was about to jump in the shower. What about you?"

"I'm on my way home now. I can't look at my computer one more second."

"Your days are just as long as mine. Have you eaten?" Vincent asked.

"Not yet, but I plan to grab something on the way home."

"Why don't you let me cook dinner for you? I'm a pretty good cook, and I would love the company," he announced.

"Are you sure? I know you're probably tired."

Vincent removed his watch and said, "I'm fine, Elizabeth. Do you know where the Vineyard Lofts are in midtown?"

"As a matter of fact, I do."

Vincent gave her instructions on where to park her car and how to get on the floor to his loft. It would give him just enough time to shower and start dinner before she arrived. He didn't know where the evening would lead, but his discussion with Cherise earlier in the day left him yearning for some female companionship.

By the time Elizabeth made it to Vincent's loft, he had showered, baked a couple of potatoes, made a salad, and was about to grill a couple of steaks. She rang the door bell.

Vincent opened the door and smiled when he saw her holding a bottle of Chardonnay.

"Thanks for inviting me over for dinner, Vincent. I brought a gift," she announced as she held the bottle up to him.

He closed the door and said, "That wasn't necessary, but thanks for accepting my dinner invitation on such short notice."

"I wouldn't have it any other way," she pointed out as she set her purse on an end table.

"Thank you, Elizabeth," he replied as he made his way back to the kitchen. "Well, this is my home. Would you like a tour?"

"Of course. It's beautiful. I love the exposed beams and the dark hardwood floors."

He took her by the hand and said, "You haven't seen anything yet."

The first stop was the kitchen, which was adorned with granite countertops and stainless steel appliances. The color scheme had burgundy and emerald green tones which gave it a masculine feel.

"Your kitchen is beautiful, Vincent, and it looks like you have dinner under control."

He pulled two wine glasses out of the cabinet then opened the wine. After pouring two glasses, he said, "I love cooking, which meant I wanted a great kitchen, but I'll have to admit that my sister-in-law helped me decorate the place."

"She has great taste."

Vincent handed his glass to Elizabeth and picked up the tray of T-bone steaks. "Follow me. I want to get these on the grill, and then we can finish the tour."

Elizabeth followed Vincent onto a large balcony, where he opened a gas grill. He turned to her and asked, "How do you like your steak?"

She sipped her wine and said, "Medium well."

"Medium well it is," he replied.

"Oh, Vincent, you have a beautiful view of the city. It's so peaceful out here, yet you get the subtle sounds of the city. I must say I'm a little envious."

He closed the lid to the grill and held out his hand for his wine glass. "You wouldn't be envious if you knew how much this view cost" he said.

She giggled and said, "I'm sure it's worth every penny."

They walked back into the loft together and made their way down the hallway. "It is worth every penny. I got in on it before the prices went up. It's a great investment, and it's close to work."

She nodded and nearly passed out when she saw his huge bedroom. Vincent had a king-size bed with a gold-and-orange comforter. Colorful pillows accented the color scheme.

"Well, what do you think?" he asked.

"Amazing."

"The bathroom is over here," he replied as he pointed to the other side of the room. The large bathroom had a jetted tub, and a two-person shower with gold faucets.

"Oh, my, this looks like something out of a magazine."

He smiled with appreciation and said, "I'm glad you like it. I'd better go check on the steaks. Make yourself at home. There's another bedroom and full bath down the hallway if you want to take a look."

"I think I will," she replied as she followed him out of his bedroom and made her way into the spare bedroom, which was decorated just as beautifully as the others.

Vincent turned the steaks over on the grill and looked out at the city lights. He felt relaxed with Elizabeth, but he couldn't help but think about Cherise and how much she meant to him.

"How are the steaks coming along?" Elizabeth asked as she rejoined Vincent on the balcony.

"They will be ready in just a second," he answered.

"Vincent, I really do love your home. Thanks for the tour."

He finished off his wine and said, "Thank you. Are you ready to eat?"

"You bet!"

Elizabeth and Vincent had finished dinner, cleaned up the kitchen, and played one game of chess. Now they sat on the sofa, enjoying great conversation talking and listening to jazz music. The wine had put both of them in a very relaxed mood, and without hesitation, he leaned over and kissed her softly on the lips. Elizabeth had been waiting for a kiss like this from Vincent, and she melted in his embrace as their kisses became even more heated. Vincent's hands caressed all the beautiful curves of her body.

Just as he was about to lead her into the bedroom, his cell phone rang, interrupting them.

Breathless, he said, "Hold that thought."

On the other end of the telephone, he listened as his nephew yelled into the phone. Vincent couldn't tell if someone was hurt or what was going on until he was finally able to calm Mase down. After excusing himself from Elizabeth, he made his way down the hallway to his bedroom so he could talk in private.

"Mase, take a deep breath and tell me what's wrong," Vincent said.

"It's my dad. He's . . . he's . . ." Mase stuttered.

"What, son? What about your dad?" Vincent pleaded with him.

"He's cheating on my mom!"

Vincent's head dropped in disbelief.

"What happened, Mase? Is your father home?"

"No, he's not here. I hate him, Unc," he yelled through his sniffles.

"No, you don't. You're just angry," Vincent replied as he

tried to calm his nephew, but it was obvious to Vincent that Mase was in a fragile state of mind.

"Where's your mother?"

Mase was almost hyperventilating at this point. "She's downstairs."

"Have you said anything to her about this?" Vincent asked.

"No, but she knows I'm pissed about something. She keeps asking me what's wrong. Can you come over, Uncle Vincent?"

"I'll be right there, Mase, and don't worry, it's going to be okay."

Vincent hung up the telephone, and anger gripped his heart. His first instinct was to track his brother down and kick his ass, but right now, his nephew needed him more, and he wasn't about to let him down. As he made his way back into the living room, he found Elizabeth standing by the door with her purse on her shoulders.

"I'm sorry, Elizabeth. I guess you can tell I have a family situation I have to deal with."

She nodded and said, "Don't worry about it. I need to be heading home anyway. I hope everything's okay."

He tucked his cell phone in his pocket and said, "Thanks. My nephew needs to talk to me."

She walked over to him and gave him a slow, sensual kiss on the lips. "Don't worry. I understand. I had a good time tonight."

Vincent grabbed his keys and said, "I did too, especially the last fifteen minutes of the evening and that kiss."

Elizabeth blushed as she walked out the door ahead of Vincent then stepped inside the elevator with him.

"Next time, dinner's on me," she announced as she pushed the button for the ground floor.

"I'm looking forward to it," he answered as the elevator

took them down to the parking garage. As the elevator doors opened, he asked, "Are you okay to drive?"

"Yes, I'm fine."

Vincent took her hand into his and said, "Come on, so I can walk you to your car."

There Vincent gave her another kiss on the lips before climbing into his own car. Their night had been interrupted, but it gave him a clear indication that there was a good chance their next date would end up between the sheets.

Vincent pulled into his brother's driveway and shut off the engine. It was a little before ten o'clock, and he wasn't sure if Cherise was aware that he was coming over. He rang the doorbell, and within seconds, she opened the door with a confused look on her face.

"What are you doing here?" She asked as she unlocked the storm door and tightened the belt on her short silk robe.

"Mase called and said he needed to talk to me about something."

"This late?" Cherise asked as she closed the door behind him.

"It sounded important," Vincent revealed as Cherise made her way over to the stairs. Before she could go up to get him, Mase appeared on the landing above them.

"Son, what is so important that you called your uncle all the way out here so late?" Cherise asked curiously.

"It's private, Momma."

She folded her arms and asked, "What do you mean, 'private'? Are you in some kind of trouble at school?"

"No, ma'am. I just needed to talk to Uncle Vincent."

Cherise turned to Vincent and asked, "Do you know what this is about?"

Vincent started up the stairs and said, "He's a teenage boy, C. J. It could be about anything. Give me a chance to talk to him. You can go on to bed. I'll lock up on my way out."

"I'm not going anywhere until I know what's going on. Knock on my door when you're finished," Cherise as she followed him up the stairs.

"Where's Janelle?" Vincent asked.

"She's supposed to be asleep, but it wouldn't surprise me if she was still up."

"Do you mind if I look in on her?" Vincent asked.

She swallowed the lump in her throat. The way Vincent was looking at her made her feel like he knew what she was hiding.

"Of course I don't. Just don't wake her."

Vincent patted Mase on the shoulders and said, "Go on into your room. I'll be there in a second. I just want to look in on your sister first."

Mase nodded and entered his bedroom, closing the door behind him. Cherise stood in the hallway and watched as Vincent slowly opened the door to Janelle's room. She was asleep, so he quietly made his way over to her bed, leaned down and kissed her on the forehead. His heart fluttered from the loving contact. It was an electrifying connection and it made his heart thump in his chest. After staring at her angelic face for a few seconds, he eased out of her room and gently closed the bedroom door. He turned to Cherise and whispered, "She looks like an angel."

Tears rolled down Cherise's cheek, threatening to give away her secret. As she wiped them away, she said, "She's a true gift from God. They both are."

"I know," he replied. "What's up with the tears?"

"I'm just worried about Mase," she explained. "He's been

quiet and closed off in his room ever since I got home, acting like he's mad at the world."

"Where's Mason?" Vincent asked as he leaned against the wall.

"At work," she answered as she wiped away a few more tears. "I thought he would've been home by now. Sometimes it's like he's working undercover all over again."

Vincent walked over to her and smiled. Cherise wrapped her arms around his waist and hugged him tightly. Her body was tense, but it felt heavenly against his, and it was only natural for him to embrace her as well. No words were spoken, because no words needed to be spoken. They just held each other and listened to the rhythm of their heart beats.

When he finally released her, he whispered, "Do me a favor and wait for me downstairs."

Unable to answer, she nodded then began walking down the stairs.

Inside Mase's bedroom, Vincent took a seat in a chair and said, "Okay, what has you so upset?"

Mase looked into Vincent's eyes and began telling him about the text messages. Mase remembered every word, and even included the ones from Cherise, just to compare them from the unknown sender.

"Mase, you can't determine anything from a text message."

"Come on, Unc! If he wasn't cheating, why would he be texting with another woman?"

Vincent took Mase by the hands and said, "Mase, I know you're angry and hurt right now over what you saw today, but don't you think you need to talk to your dad first before you draw any conclusions? Those texts could be work related."

Frustrated, Mase replied, "That's some bullshit, Unc! Those text messages were the kind you get from a girlfriend, and they can't be work related, because he doesn't work undercover anymore. Remember?"

Mase had a point. There was no reason Mason should be perpetrating with a mark. Cold cases were his division now, and receiving suggestive messages from another woman was unnecessary.

Vincent was becoming frustrated. He was trying to defend Mason, but Mase was blowing every one of his excuses out of the water.

"Mase, I would appreciate it if you wouldn't use that kind of language when you talk to me. I know you're pissed, but try to hold yourself together."

"I'm sorry," Mase apologized. "It's just that sometimes I wish my dad would be around more and just be a regular dad."

Vincent took a breath to calm down before speaking. "Mase, your father is going through a departmental transition from undercover to cold cases. He's still under a lot of stress, so give him a chance to explain the text messages before you think the worst of him. He loves you guys and will do anything for you."

"You've been more of a dad than he ever has. He's never around, and he loves his job more than he loves us."

Vincent listened quietly as Mase reminded him of all the ballgames and family functions his father had missed, and just being at home at night to give them the security most children expected growing up. Vincent understood Mase's pain, but he still did his best to show his nephew that his father loved him in spite of his choices.

"Mase, your father is a cop. I'm a cop. That's all he wanted to be growing up. It's what we do, but it doesn't mean that you, your sister, or your mother mean less to him than his job. Yes, he's missed some important events in your lives, but we all have, even your mother," he explained. "None of us are innocent of mistakes, and your father has sacrificed a lot to keep you guys safe and give you a good life, so cut him a break, okay?"

Mase picked up his basketball and threw it across the room, causing it to make a loud thump as it hit against the inside wall of his closet.

"He's made my mom cry for the last time. If he doesn't want to be here, he needs to go on with that woman so Momma can find somebody to make her happy."

"Are you listening to me?" Vincent asked. "Do you have any idea what dangerous situations your father has put himself in to get thugs that could kill you off the streets?"

"Yes, I do, Unc!" Mase yelled.

Vincent stood and angrily said, "No, son, I don't think you do!"

Vincent decided to tell Mase about some of the dangerous cases Mason had worked. If Mase wanted to act like a man, he was going to talk to him like one. He wasn't condoning Mason's exchange of text messages with another woman, but until the truth was revealed, he didn't want Mase judging his father.

Once he finished telling him about some of the cases Mason had worked, Mase was holding his head in his hands. He had no idea how deep undercover his father had been, and now seemed to have a newfound respect for him. When he looked up at his uncle, he had tears in his eyes.

"I just don't want to see my mother cry anymore."

Vincent patted Mase on the shoulders and said, "Your mother is a tough lady. She can handle your father, so don't worry about her, okay?"

Mase nodded in agreement and Vincent gave him a hug.

"Talk to your dad about the texts and tell him how you feel. If you want me to be there, I will. Now, go to bed and don't breathe a word of this to your mother."

"What are you going to tell her?" Mase asked. "She knows something's going on."

Vincent walked to the door and said, "I'll just tell her it's girl trouble. Cool?"

A smile finally graced his face as he bragged, "I don't have any problems with girls, Unc."

He chuckled and said, "I know you don't. You're a McKenzie."

"True that. Thanks for coming over and talking to me, Unc."

Vincent opened the bedroom door and said, "I'm here for you anytime, so don't ever hesitate to call me. Good night."

"Good night."

Vincent closed the door and made his way downstairs, where he found Cherise in the family room, watching the news. She looked up at him and asked, "What's going on with Mase?"

He walked over to her and said, "He's okay. He just wanted to talk to me about a girl."

"A girl? What girl?" Cherise asked.

"Calm down, C. J. He just had some questions and concerns about a girl."

"Oh my God! Is he having sex?" Cherise asked as she put her hand over her heart.

"I don't think so, but don't worry. He knows the dos and don'ts with girls. Mason spoke to him, and so did I," Vincent explained. "He's definitely interested in girls, but sports are still number one on his list."

"Are you sure?" she asked. "You know he looks much older than he really is. Those older girls are always hanging on him. I'm afraid they might be pressuring him into having sex."

Vincent chuckled and said, "You know he's at that age where his hormones are popping, but I think when the time comes and he's seriously thinking about doing it, he'll say something."

"I don't even want to think about it," Cherise replied.

Vincent smiled mischievously and asked, "Are you worried about him having your level of passion and sexuality?"

"Shut up, Vincent."

He chuckled and then said, "He's a McKenzie, C. J. He'll be fine, so stop worrying."

"I'll try," she replied.

"Look, I'd better go. It's getting late and you need to go to bed."

Cherise walked him to the door and stepped out onto the porch in the cool night air. "Thanks for coming over. I hope Mase's call didn't interrupt your evening."

He looked over at her curiously and asked, "What do you mean, like a date or something?"

Cherise didn't respond, but he could tell her curiosity was getting to her, so he decided to put her out of her misery. "It's okay. She understands that my family comes first."

There was an awkward silence between the two for a few seconds before Cherise spoke.

"Is it getting serious?"

He smiled and then slowly walked over to her.

"Look at you, all up in my business. What do you really want to know, C. J.? Do you want to know if I've slept with her?"

Embarrassed, she turned to walk back into the house. "Like you said, it's none of my business."

He grabbed her hand, stopping her, and spun her around to face him. "Are you jealous?"

"No, I'm not jealous," she answered in defense. "You're free to date and sleep with whoever you want to."

Vincent knew she was jealous. It showed all over her face. He took a step back from her and with sheer honesty, said, "I know it's wrong for me to say this, but I want you so bad right now I can hardly breathe. You need to go back into the house before I lose control."

His confession sent shivers all over her body, and she remembered a time in her life when she would've taken him up on his offer without giving it a second thought. Her lower body began to throb as the sensuality of his words sunk in. The sad thing was that Vincent's love for her had always been obvious, but her husband's love was sometimes questionable. Unable to speak or respond, she stepped back inside the house and locked the door behind her.

Chapter Six

Mason drove Janelle and Mase to their grandparents' home to spend the night. It was the day of his birthday party, and he was looking forward to spending time with his close friends. Once he pulled into the Jernigans' driveway, Janelle kissed her father on the cheek and immediately jumped out of his car. She ran up to her grandmother, who was waiting for them on the porch.

Mason exited the vehicle and asked, "What's your hurry, Janelle?"

"Granddaddy's taking me to a ballgame."

"I see," he replied as he gave his mother-in-law a loving hug. "Hello, Patricia. Thanks for watching the kids for us tonight."

"They're our grandchildren, Mason. We love having them over. Cherise has been working hard on your party. I hope you guys have fun tonight."

He playfully tugged on Janelle's ear and said, "I'm sure we will."

"Why is Mase still sitting in the car?" she asked.

Mason turned and said, "I don't know. I'll go get him. Give us a call if·you need us."

She opened the door for Janelle to enter the house ahead of her, and said, "Oh, we'll be fine. Tell Cherise to give me a call tomorrow."

"I will," he answered as he made his way back over to his

car. He opened the car door and climbed in behind the steering wheel. When he looked over at Mase, he seemed to be in a trance as he stared out the passenger's side window.

"Mase, are you planning on staying with your grandparents tonight?"

His son turned to him and asked, "Why are you getting text messages from another woman?"

Mason felt as if a cinder block had been thrown against his chest. How could he know, and what exactly did he know?

"What are you talking about, son?"

"Come on, Dad. You know exactly what I'm talking about. I read the text messages in your phone."

Mason lowered his head and asked, "What are you doing going through my cell phone?"

"Are you upset that I went through your messages, or that I found out about your girlfriend?"

"Now, wait just a damn minute, Mase. You will not talk to me with that kind of tone," he chastised. "I can see you're upset, but I do not have a girlfriend. I love your mother."

Tears spilled out of Mase's eyes. He didn't believe his father because he read the messages and his father's replies, and they were obviously between two illicit lovers.

"I don't believe you."

Mason reached over and put his hand on his son's shoulder to comfort him.

"Mase, I'm your father, so I'm going to be honest with you. I don't know who sent those text messages to me, and now I know it was a bad decision on my part to reply to them. I only did it to try to find out who they were from. I am not cheating on your mother."

"But you have before, haven't you?" Mason asked abruptly.

His father sighed and lowered his head again before speaking. "You're not a child anymore, so I feel like I can talk to you man to man. I'll admit that I've done some things in my past that hurt your mother, and I regret them with all my heart. I was a different person then, and life between your mother and I was under a lot of strain. Things are better now, and I would never do anything to hurt her again."

"So, you have had a girlfriend before?" Mase asked.

"Yes," he answered as he hugged his son's neck. "And I promise I'll never hurt your mother like that again."

Mase wiped away his tears and asked, "Are you serious, Dad?"

"I promise, son, and if it's the last thing I do, I'm going to find out who's sending me the messages so I can put a stop to it."

Mase lowered his head and said, "I told Uncle Vincent about the text messages. I was pissed and needed to talk to somebody, so I called him."

"That's okay, Mase. I want you to be able to go to your uncle if I'm not around. Does your mother know?"

He shook his head and then said, "Uncle Vincent told me not to tell her."

"Your uncle told you the right thing, son. There's no reason to upset your mother unnecessarily. I'll get to the bottom of it, so you don't have to worry about this anymore, okay?"

"Yes, sir."

"Good. Now, wipe away those tears and go on inside with your sister. If you want to, we can talk about this some more tomorrow."

Mase opened the door and climbed out of the vehicle. As he walked up the sidewalk, Mason said, "I love you, Mase."

"I love you too, Dad."

***

Later that evening, Mason's party kicked off as planned. The backyard was decorated with Chinese lanterns, and the pool was filled with floating candles. Under a small tent, the caterers decorated the buffet table with several delicacies, including chilled shrimp, fresh herb roasted crostini, skewers of melon, mozzarella, and prosciutto. The McKenzies served a variety of wines, beer, and non-alcoholic beverages. The backyard was full of their closest friends, and Cherise couldn't be happier.

Cherise was dressed in a sheer lavender blouse and white pants, while Mason was dressed casually in dark gray slacks and a light blue button-down shirt. The couple was overjoyed at the outpouring of love from his friends, and the gift table was full.

As the DJ played one old school jam after another, Cherise didn't even notice when Vincent and Elizabeth arrived. When she did, she could see that Elizabeth was very beautiful and was clinging somewhat to Vincent. As she studied her from afar, she noticed her designer spaghetti-strapped tie-dye dress and perfectly manicured toes and nails. Vincent was as handsome as ever, and his clothes always fit him like a male model. Tonight he was dressed in tan linen slacks and a brown shirt. It wasn't long before they made their way over to Cherise near the buffet table.

Vincent kissed Cherise on the cheek and said, "Hey, C. J. You look beautiful, as always."

"Thank you, Vincent."

"Elizabeth, this is my sister-in-law, Cherise. Cherise, this is Elizabeth."

Elizabeth held out her hand and said, "It's nice to finally meet you. I've heard so many good things about you."

Cherise shook Elizabeth's hand and said, "It's nice to meet you as well. Make yourself at home. We have food and drinks, so enjoy."

Vincent scanned the crowd and asked, "Where's the birthday boy?"

Cherise looked over her shoulder and said, "He's over by the table, admiring his cake."

Vincent waved Mason over to join them so he could introduce him to Elizabeth. Once introductions were over, Vincent led Elizabeth over to the bartender so she could get a glass of wine before getting something to eat.

Mason hugged Cherise's waist from behind and asked, "So, what do you think? Do you like her?"

She watched the couple mingle with guests as they sipped their wine. "She's pretty, but don't you think she's clinging to Vincent?"

Mason laughed and said, "She just got here, babe, and remember, she is around a bunch of people she doesn't know. Give her a few minutes. I'm sure she'll loosen up, especially with this great music."

Cherise wrapped her arms around Mason's neck and gave him a loving kiss. "Maybe you're right. Do you want to dance, detective?"

"I'd love to," he replied just as the DJ played a slow Brian McKnight song. They were happy, and while he was still concerned that Mase had seen the text messages, he felt confident that he had put out what could've been devastating to his marriage if Cherise found out about them. Unfortunately, upstairs in their bedroom, Mason received several more strange text messages that would deepen the mystery of the unknown caller.

***

An hour later, Vincent walked over to Cherise, who was talking to one of the officers on Mason's cold case team and his wife. Vincent shook his hand and greeted him and his wife before asking if he could borrow Cherise. After a brief conversation with the couple, Vincent and Cherise walked over to the buffet table and sampled a few of the items.

"What's up, Vincent? Did your little girlfriend finally turn you a loose?"

"I see you have jokes," he replied before putting a crostini in his mouth. "Be nice."

"I am being nice. She's cute."

"Cute?" Vincent asked. "Look, I'm not even going to go there. Come dance with me."

Cherise linked her arm with Vincent as they walked toward the dancing area. "I was wondering when you was going to ask."

He pulled her into his arms and said, "It's all about timing, sweetheart. There was no way I was going to leave here tonight without dancing with you."

She smiled.

Vincent looked over at Mason, who was talking to Elizabeth. "Mason looks happy. He's having a great time."

Cherise looked over at Mason and Elizabeth and said, "That's all I want. He deserved the party. He's been working so hard lately."

Vincent pulled her closer to his body and said, "So have you."

"I'm good," she replied as she looked up into his eyes. "Thanks again for helping with the decorations."

The song ended, and Vincent reluctantly released her. "You know I'll do anything for you."

"I know," she answered. "You're the best, Vincent."

"Listen, while we're talking, I'm sorry about what I said the other night. Even though I meant every word of it, I was out of line."

She swallowed the lump in her throat and said, "Don't worry about it. No harm done."

"Good."

Cherise took a step back and said, "Well, I guess you'd better get back over to Elizabeth before she comes running across the yard to scratch my eyes out."

He laughed out loud and said, "It's not that serious, C. J."

Before she walked away, she said, "That's what you say. Be careful."

Vincent watched Cherise's curvy backside as she walked into the house to check on the caterers, and it stirred him physically. When he turned his attention back to Elizabeth, she was staring at him. Mason was no longer with her, and if his instincts were on target, he saw jealousy in her eyes.

When he made his way over to her, he smiled and asked, "Are you having a good time?"

"Yes," she replied. "Their home is beautiful, and your brother has a great sense of humor."

Vincent sat down next to her just as a caterer walked past him with a tray of beers. Vincent helped himself to a bottle and said, "Yeah, he's a real comedian."

Elizabeth sat quietly next to him as they watched a small group of people step to an R. Kelly song.

"Are you a stepper?" Vincent asked.

"I've done it a few times."

He pointed toward the dancers and asked, "Why don't you join them? They're having a lot of fun."

She turned to him and said, "I was hoping to get a slow dance with you first."

"That's without a doubt, and the next time the DJ plays one, it's me and you."

Elizabeth smiled and then stepped into an area that made Vincent very uncomfortable.

"Your sister-in-law is stunning, and she looks happy with her husband, but I couldn't help but notice that you guys seem to be very close as well."

Vincent looked over at her curiously and asked, "What do you mean?"

She fumbled with her words and her hands. Before speaking, she let out a nervous laugh and said, "You and your sister-in-law seem very close."

"We are," he replied.

"I could tell by the way you look at her."

That particular comment got Vincent's attention. He looked over at her, set his beer down on the table, and asked, "And what way is that?"

"You know, like you have feelings for her," she revealed.

He looked Elizabeth directly in the eyes and said something she never expected.

"I do have feelings for her. Strong feelings," he admitted. "Elizabeth, there are things you don't know about me and my family, and for now, I prefer to keep it that way. Like I told you before, we're a family of civil servants, which means we've been through some serious shit. Some of the things were so horrible it would tear most families apart, so don't step to me about things you have no clue about."

Elizabeth had witnessed a taste of Vincent's anger, and now she regretted ever bringing up her observation. She couldn't do anything but apologize the best way she knew how.

"I'm sorry, Vincent, and forget I ever said anything about your sister-in-law. It's a wonderful night with good music and delicious food. I don't want to blow it by making a stupid remark."

Vincent wasn't buying her apology, even though their parents raised them to forgive. He was angry, and he didn't care about letting her know as he stood and picked up his beer. "Elizabeth, I like you, I really do, but your comment pissed me off. We're just friends. Don't get it twisted."

Before Elizabeth could apologize again, he walked across the yard and into the house, leaving her alone, with tears stinging her eyes. Needing a drink, she walked over to the bartender and ordered a mojito and quickly swallowed it. As soon as she set the glass down, she ordered another one, and drank it down even faster. The bartender was mesmerized, and suggested that she take it slow. Just as she was about to order another one, a gentleman asked her to dance, and she happily accepted.

Inside the house, Vincent found a seat alone in the family room. Mason caught a glimpse of him as he walked past him on the way up to his bedroom, so he stopped to find out why he was sitting in the house.

"Hey, bro. Why are you in here all by yourself? Are you okay?"

Vincent drained the beer and then said, "Yeah, I'm good. I'm just taking a little breather. Where are you headed?"

"Up to the bedroom to get a picture of the kids that Cherise wants to show somebody."

"Cool," Vincent replied nonchalantly. "Listen, before you go, I need to talk to you about Mase."

Mason walked farther into the family room and said, "Yeah, he told me he talked to you about some text messages he found on my cell."

"What's going on, Mason?"

"Nothing's going on," he explained. "I don't know who's sending me those messages, but I intend to find out. I hate that my son saw them, but I'm glad he came to you instead of telling Cherise about it. He loves and respects you so much."

Vincent stood and said, "I love him too, and you'd better get to the bottom of this before it gets out of hand. I hope it's just somebody joking around with you, but you and I both know that you have a lot of ladies in your past, so it could be any of them trying to make trouble for you."

He waved Vincent off and said, "Don't remind me. That's behind me now. Cherise is the only woman I love."

Mason's expression of love for his wife hit Vincent hard in the stomach, but it wasn't like he didn't already know about it.

"Now, back to you. Tell me the real reason you're hiding out in here."

Coming clean, Vincent smiled and said, "Elizabeth said something that pissed me off."

Mason sat on the arm of the sofa and asked, "About what?"

Frustrated and not wanting to reveal the gist of the conversation, Vincent said, "Honestly, she's making me feel a little pressured. She's cool, but that's as far as I'm going to let it go right now."

Mason stood and said, "You've charmed her, little brother. Go kiss and make up. I'm sure, whatever it was she said, you can get past it. Besides, it's my birthday party, and I refuse to have you walking around here with your ass tight."

Vincent laughed. "You're ignorant."

"I know," he replied as he hugged his brother before walking toward the hallway. "Now, go make up with Elizabeth."

Mason made it sound easy to make up with Elizabeth, but Vincent was still fuming. Even though she was correct in picking up on his emotional attachment to Cherise, she was wrong for calling him on it. Now his decision was to do what Mason said and make up with her, or continue to be angry.

Just as he was about to go back out into the yard, Cherise walked into the family room and said, "Mason told me that you and Elizabeth had an argument."

"Stay out of it, C. J."

She pointed toward the backyard and said, "She don't know anyone here, and you left her out there all by herself. What are you arguing about anyway?"

He brushed past Cherise and calmly said, "You."

"Me? What about me?" she asked as she followed him out of the family room and into the kitchen. Before she could get an answer, she was interrupted by one of the caterers.

Minutes later, Cherise found him slow dancing with Elizabeth. She appeared to have a smile on her face, so maybe they had made up. If that was the case, it still had her wondering what the argument was about in the first place. Regardless of the reason, she didn't want anything or anybody to ruin Mason's party.

A few hours later, the party was over and Cherise and Mason thanked their guests for their attendance and gifts. Inside the house, the caterers packed up the leftovers so Cherise could put them away. In the backyard, Vincent assisted the DJ in breaking down his equipment, while Elizabeth helped gather the table linens and candles off the tables. Once all the guests were gone, Mason started boxing up the bottles of wine and beer so they could be taken into the house.

Elizabeth walked into the kitchen with a handful of candles and asked, "Where would you like me to put these candles, Cherise?"

She pointed toward the garage door and said, "There's a box on the utility shelf right outside the door."

Elizabeth put the candles in the box and returned to the kitchen. "Is there anything else you need me to do?"

Cherise stacked a couple of Tupperware containers on top of each other and said, "You've already done more than enough. Thank you, but you're a guest."

"I don't mind helping," Elizabeth replied as she pulled out a chair and sat down at the island. "It doesn't look like Vincent's ready to go anyway."

Cherise looked toward the backyard and noticed that Vincent and Mason were still helping the bartender and DJ.

"There's no reason for you guys to hang around. I'm sure you're tired. I know I am."

Elizabeth smiled and said, "It was a nice party. I'm glad Vincent invited me, even though he's a little upset with me right now."

Cherise glanced up at Elizabeth before opening the refrigerator and said, "I'm sorry."

She waved Cherise off and said, "It's okay. He deserves to be a little angry with me. I shouldn't have said what I said."

Cherise could tell that Elizabeth was trying to bait her, but as bad as she wanted to know what their argument was about, she wasn't going to talk about it with her. She picked up the Tupperware containers and headed for the basement. Before walking down the stairs, Cherise said, "I'm sure it'll work out."

Downstairs, Cherise put the food in their spare refrigerator and then started moving boxes back in place that were somehow blocking the aisle. That's when Mason joined her with the box of leftover wine and champagne.

"Is there any more room in the refrigerator?" Mason asked.

"Sure, honey," Cherise replied as she held the refrigerator door open for him.

Once he finished placing the bottles on the bottom row, he stood and said, "Vincent and Elizabeth are getting ready to leave."

"Good," she replied. "I'm ready to call it a night."

Mason headed up the stairs and said, "Me too, so hurry up so I can thank you properly for the party."

She giggled and said, "I'll be right up. I think I have a few more containers of food to bring down, and we need to get the gifts and bring them inside."

"I'll get them to help so we can finish up."

Seconds later, as Cherise leaned into the refrigerator to make more room, she heard footsteps coming down the stairs. "Babe, ask Vincent if he wants to take any of the leftovers or cake home."

"Ask me yourself," Vincent replied, startling her. She looked down at his large hands and noticed him holding three more Tupperware containers.

"I thought you were Mason."

Vincent slid the containers into the refrigerator and laughed. "He told me to bring these down to you."

Cherise closed the refrigerator and asked, "Where's your girlfriend?"

"I see you're trying to be funny," he answered with a smile. "Elizabeth, who is not my girlfriend, is helping Mason bring in the gifts."

"I'm sorry, Vincent. I couldn't resist. I'm just teasing you. She seems nice. I hope you're not still mad at her."

He rubbed his chin and said, "We'll work it out."

Cherise stared at him for a second before taking a step toward the stairs. He was a wonderful and loving man, and her heart still carried a big part of him. Whenever they were alone, it was difficult for them to ignore the strong connection between them, no matter how hard they tried to deny it. Tonight was no different.

"Vincent, I want to thank you again for all your help with the party. I couldn't have done it by myself."

Vincent took her by the hand and pulled her closer. "I didn't mind."

Her perfume was mesmerizing, and the heat from her body felt heavenly. Cherise closed her eyes as they embraced each other lovingly. He could feel her heart beating against his own at the same rhythm.

"I miss this," she whispered, causing his body to instantly react. She hadn't held him this way in a long time, and she had to admit it felt wonderful. They'd been so careful with their relationship the past few months, so Mason wouldn't have any reason not to trust them. In the meantime, they stopped allowing themselves to be friends.

He looked down into her eyes. He was glad she was allowing herself to be natural and familiar with him. It could've been the champagne she had consumed, but he hoped it was all Cherise McKenzie, the woman he fell in love with many years ago. Either way, he was just glad she let him get close to her again.

"I've missed this too," he replied. He didn't want to release her, and she didn't seem to want to release him. He knew he wouldn't be able to hold her like this much longer without succumbing to the urge to kiss her, and that could be disastrous, especially if Mason caught them.

"Can I tell you something?" he asked her softly.

"Sure, Vincent," she replied as she reached up and caressed his face.

He leaned down close to her ear and whispered, "I love you, and I will always love you."

She kissed him on the chin and said, "I'll always love you too."

Vincent smiled and kissed her tenderly on the cheek before releasing her. "You've made my night, C. J. Thank you, and have a good night."

She watched him as he headed toward the stairs, neither noticing a shadow on the landing, slowly backing away. Someone had obviously heard their conversation.

Forty-five minutes later, Vincent dropped Elizabeth off at home after somewhat of a quiet ride to her house. He did slightly apologize to her for getting so angry earlier, but he explained to her once again not to rush their relationship. Elizabeth also apologized and agreed not to rush. Before departing, Vincent thanked her with a warm hug and peck on the lips for accompanying him to the party.

Later that night, Cherise and Mason showered and then made love like college students on spring break. Both of them were highly charged with love and passion from their own private source of inspiration.

Downtown, Vincent tossed and turned in his bed by his own choosing before falling asleep just as the sun began to rise.

Chapter Seven

The next morning, Cherise woke up to an empty bed. When she looked at the clock, it was nearly noon, but she deserved to sleep in, a luxury not often offered to her. After gathering her thoughts, she sat up in bed and then made her way into the bathroom, to shower and brush her teeth. Still somewhat tired from the previous night, she slowly dressed in sweats and a T-shirt and headed downstairs to find Mason.

Outside on the patio, Mason scanned through his cell phone at the latest series of text messages and voicemails. Some were so erotic that he had no choice but to delete them so Cherise wouldn't find them.

"Hey, baby," she greeted him, startling him so much that he dropped his phone.

Cherise picked up the phone and handed it to him. "I'm sorry, sweetheart. I didn't mean to sneak up on you. Are you okay?"

Mason accepted the cell phone and said, "Yeah, it's just that I didn't hear you come out the door."

"You did seem to be in deep thought," she replied before taking a sip of her Mimosa. "What were you concentrating so hard on?"

"My phone," he answered. "I was just checking my messages."

Cherise sat in his lap and glanced down at his cell phone.

Mason looked into her eyes and asked, "Is that orange juice?"

"No, it's a Mimosa. Do you want some?"

"Nah, go ahead."

Cherise snatched the phone out of his hand and threatened to throw it in the pool.

"You promised you wouldn't work on your day off."

He reached for the cell phone and said, "Come on, babe. Stop playing."

"It's going in the pool if you don't put it away."

He playfully stood with her in his arms and said, "If you throw my phone in the pool, you're going in right behind it."

"You wouldn't," she challenged him.

He kissed her slowly on the lips and then asked, "Do you really want to tempt me?"

Mason had thrown her in the pool before, and since she had a fresh hairstyle, she wasn't about to call his bluff. She gave in and handed him the phone.

He laughed and said, "Sucker."

"I'm not trying to mess up my 'do," she replied before taking another sip.

Just then, Mason got a text. Concerned that it could be another erotic message, he ignored it.

"Aren't you going to check your text?" she asked.

He slid it into his pocket and said, "You said no work today, so no work."

"Thank you, baby. Have you talked to the kids this morning?"

"Not yet," he replied. "We're still going over there for dinner, aren't we?"

She sat down in the chair and sighed. "To be honest, Mason, I don't feel like moving an inch today. If you want to go, it's fine, but I think I'm going to pass. I'm not very hungry anyway."

Mason's cell phone vibrated in his pocket, alerting him to another message. Once again, he ignored it.

"You might not be hungry now, but you will be later."

Cherise glanced down at his pocket and said, "Sounds like you got another text. Somebody's really trying to reach you."

He smiled and then pulled the cell phone back out of his pocket. This time, he turned it off.

"They can try all they want to. I'm turning it off so we'll have no more interruptions."

She finished off the rest of her cocktail and said, "If it was urgent, they know to call the house."

"You're right. Now, back to dinner. If you don't go over to your parents' house for dinner, Patricia's going to be all over me about you."

"I'll call her later," she stated as she stood and took him by the hand, leading him toward the door. "Let's go open up your gifts."

"Don't you want the kids to be here for that?"

They entered the kitchen and Cherise opened the refrigerator and made herself another Mimosa. "We don't have to open all of them, just a few."

Mason nodded in agreement, but before he could leave the kitchen, the house telephone rang.

"Hello?"

A female voice whispered, "Did you get my gift, baby?"

"Excuse me?" Mason responded. "Speak up. I can barely hear you."

"Read my text, baby," the voice whispered before hanging up.

Mason realized who the caller was. He was stunned. With Cherise in the room, he had to play it cool, so he answered, "Okay," before hanging up the receiver.

Cherise looked over at Mason and asked, "Who is it, babe?"

He hung up the telephone and lied. "It's nothing, just the pharmacy calling to let me know that my pain medicine is ready to be picked up. Can we hold off opening the gifts until later? I need to run to the pharmacy."

"Is your back bothering you again?" she asked, clearly concerned.

"Some days are worse than others, but I'll be okay. I might have to have that surgery, but I'm trying to put it off."

She massaged his lower back before planting a kiss on his lips. "I'm sorry, babe. Maybe we overdid things last night."

"No, we didn't overdo it," he answered, speaking of their intimate tryst the night before. "In fact, it was long overdue. Besides, I enjoyed myself, and I hope you did too."

Cherise massaged her husband's lower back lovingly and said, "We're going to have to take it easy. I keep forgetting that your back is still fragile."

Months earlier, Vincent saved their lives by knocking them to the floor, shielding their body with his, and taking the bullet meant for them. Mason fell down in an awkward position, hitting his back against a piece of furniture. He'd had back problems ever since.

"Maybe you should lie down and let me go pick up your prescription."

He kissed her forehead and said, "I'm fine. You said yourself that you were tired, so maybe you're the one who should lie down. Don't worry. I won't be long."

"Okay. Be careful."

"I will," he replied as he grabbed his keys, kissed her, and slowly exited the house. Cherise watched from the window as he backed out of the garage and disappeared down the street.

***

In a nearby park, Mason pulled into a parking space and quickly pulled out his cell phone. He turned the power back on and started reading one text after another.

HEY, BABY, I HOPE YOU LIKE MY GIFT. I WISH I COULD SEE YOUR FACE WHEN YOU OPEN IT. BY THE WAY . . . NICE PARTY LAST NIGHT. LOVE AND KISSES.

MASON, SEND ME A TEXT BACK TO LET ME KNOW YOU GOT MY MESSAGE.

SWEETHEART, YOU'RE MAKING ME FEEL ABANDONED. I LOVE YOU. TEXT BACK.

NOW YOU'RE PISSING ME OFF. DON'T MAKE ME DO SOMETHING I DON'T WANT TO DO.

By all indication, if the woman behind the text messages and phone call was who he thought it was, things could go from bad to worse real quick, even though there were many female acquaintances in his past. This woman had apparently driven by their house last night, since she knew about the party. The realization hit him that this was serious; it wasn't a prank after all. Who knows what kind of gift she had sent to his house. The last thing he needed was for one of the kids to open a gift that could possibly have something inside that would damage his marriage or tarnish their image of him.

Trying to stay calm, he sent a text back, asking the woman to meet him. Since he wasn't one hundred percent sure who she was, he'd have to tread lightly until he was sure.

HEY, BABE, WE'LL HOOK UP IN DUE TIME. IN THE MEANTIME, ENJOY MY GIFT UNTIL WE CAN ENJOY EACH OTHER. SMOOCHES!

Mason cursed and then pulled out of the park and headed to the pharmacy. This was going to be a lot more difficult that he thought. His main concern was finding out which gift at home contained God knows what from the mysterious woman. If the gift was going to be something questionable, he wanted to find out before the children returned home. If it was something indecent, he'd rather defend himself in private with Cherise than in front of the kids.

***

Mason returned home within thirty minutes with his prescription. Cherise saw the concerned expression on his face and immediately asked, "What's wrong?"

He set the prescription on the countertop and took her by the hand, leading her into the family room. He didn't want to alert her unnecessarily, because whoever was sending the text obviously wanted to hurt his marriage, but he couldn't let her.

"Mason? What's wrong?" Cherise asked again.

It was now or never, and he just wanted to get through it and move on. The couple walked into the family room, and Mason found four gifts which didn't have nametags on the outside.

"Sweetheart, I got a text from a woman who said she sent me a gift."

Cherise frowned and asked, "What woman?"

"I don't know, but whoever it is thinks it's funny. I want you to know that nothing's going on."

Without answering him, Cherise ripped open the first unmarked gift and found out it was a designer shirt and tie from one of his partners and wife. The second unmarked gift was a gift card to Home Depot, a gift from a childhood friend. The third gift was a beautiful leather wallet and an engraved keychain from Vincent. He never put his name on the outside of gifts because he always put a beautiful card on the inside.

The last gift didn't have a card, but it was wrapped beautifully. When Mason opened the box, he froze, and so did Cherise. Inside the box were an expensive pair of pink women's panties, six condoms, a bottle of Chanel perfume, a hotel key card, and a sex toy. Mason was stunned just as much as Cherise, because the items in the box all but confirmed who his admirer was. He had hoped that the notion of a sensual gift was a hoax, but all evidence in front of them proved differently.

"Son of a bitch," he mumbled, clearly taken aback by the items.

Cherise saw a small pink card in the box and quickly grabbed it so she could read it.

Happy birthday, Mason. I hope you like my gift.

You always do. You know what to do. See you soon.

Mason saw Cherise's expression go from shock to anger, and he realized that whatever was on the note had to be worse than the gift itself.

"Who sent this to you?" she asked.

"I don't know," he lied.

"You don't know? You have to know something. A woman just doesn't send a man a gift like this unless something's going on. Who is she, Mason? I'm not going to ask you again."

He set the box on the floor and said, "I'm telling you the truth. I don't know anything about this, and before you go there, I'm not having an affair."

Cherise didn't believe a word of it. She threw the card in his face and yelled, "You haven't changed one bit."

"It's the truth!" he yelled in his defense.

Cherise kicked the box, knocking it into a nearby wall as she screamed obscenities.

"No wonder you were concentrating on your cell phone so hard," she yelled at him. "Has she been calling you too?"

"She's been sending me text messages," he admitted.

"How long has this been going on?" she yelled at him.

Mason followed her out into the hallway and grabbed her by the wrist, spinning her around to face him.

"The text messages just started, but nothing's going on!" he screamed back at her as he pinned her against the wall. "I'm not cheating on you."

"What kind of text messages?" she asked.

"Seductive ones," he revealed. "I deleted them because I thought it was a joke."

"Well, obviously it's not," she replied. "Let me go, Mason."

"I'm not letting you go until you listen to me."

That's when all bad memories from their past came flooding back to her. The secret phone calls, late nights, and lies to cover his tracks.

Mason's heart pounded in his chest as he leaned into her. He didn't want to let his wife go. He felt like if he did, he would never see her again, but he was hurting her, and that was the last thing he wanted to do.

"You're hurting my arms," she whispered as tears streamed down her face.

Mason released her wrists, but immediately embraced her so she couldn't walk away.

"Sweetheart, I'm not about that anymore. I was a different person then," he stated as he cupped her face.

"You never loved me. It's always been about those whores," she replied as she pushed past him and headed up the stairs.

"I do love you!" he yelled before following her up the stairs and into their bedroom. "You're all I ever wanted. If I didn't, I wouldn't be here."

She made her way toward the bathroom, but before entering, she turned to him with her finger pointed and said, "Stop lying, Mason. It's obvious that you've made a very strong impression on one of your bitches, so until you know who and what you want, stay away from me."

He shoved his hands in his pockets in silence. The next thing he knew, he said something that would take their argument to another level. "I could say the same thing about you and Vincent."

Livid over his remark, Cherise glared at him before walking over to him. "You didn't give a damn about me until you found out I was sleeping with Vincent. Until then, as long as you were able to go and come as you pleased with those whores, it didn't matter to you what I did or who I did it with."

"He's my brother, Cherise!"

"Yes, he is!" she screamed back at him. "And if you loved me anywhere close to the way he loves me, we wouldn't be having this conversation."

Mason sat down on the side of the bed and started laughing, causing Cherise to wonder what he found so funny all of a sudden. He stopped laughing and said, "This is stupid."

"Stupid?" she asked. "My husband receives an erotic gift from another woman and I'm not supposed to be upset?"

"No! You have every right to be upset, but what about me? I know you still have feelings for Vincent. How do you think that makes me feel?"

Cherise knew Mason was still a little uneasy about her relationship with Vincent, and honestly, he had a right to be. She loved him, and always would.

"I made a bad decision with Vincent, but have you forgotten that everybody knew about you and those women but me? Have you forgotten how you were out in public more with that D.A. than you were with me? Have you forgotten about the weeks you were supposed to be working undercover when you were laid up with that woman? You didn't touch me, or even act as if I existed. How long did you expect me to sit here in this house all alone with your son asking me when you were coming home? What did you think was going to happen?"

"He's my brother, Cherise."

Mason had a valid point. She'd been a hypocrite, so quick to jump down his throat when she'd allowed herself to be emotionally and physically aroused by the mere presence of Vincent. It also didn't help the fact that she continued to conceal a life-altering secret that could definitely wreak havoc in all three of their lives forever.

She pointed her finger at him and said, "I was hurt, embarrassed, and in pain! If it hadn't been him, it would've been somebody else. You made things happen between me and Vincent, not me."

He put his hands up in defense and said, "Enough! Look, I know I'm guilty of all of the above, but the bottom line is that I want this marriage to survive. But if you're going to call me out every time someone from my past comes around, we're not going to make it."

Cherise stared at Mason and noticed the tears welling up in his eyes. She wanted to trust and believe him, but this incident didn't help matters.

"I want this marriage to work too, Mason, but you're going to have to be honest with me. Is there anything, and I mean anything, that you need to tell me that I don't know?" she asked.

He took her by the hand and gave it a gentle squeeze. "No. I told you that life is behind me. I love you, Cherise."

"I believe you, Mason, and I never meant to hurt you. I'm sorry."

He stood and pulled Cherise up into his arms to comfort her. As he wiped away her tears, he poured his heart out to her in a way he had never done before.

"I never meant to hurt you either. You're my wife, and my family means everything to me, Vincent included. So, whoever this woman is, she's out of luck. I love you."

"I love you too, Mason."

He kissed her and said, "Don't worry, babe. I'll get to the bottom of the text messages and the gift."

Cherise nodded in agreement and then disappeared into the bathroom.

Mason was emotionally drained, but he couldn't relax. Without telling Cherise where he was going, he ran downstairs, grabbed his keys, and quickly drove off.

Chapter Eight

Vincent's body was still very sensitive from the close contact with Cherise. It was as if he had been jolted with an electrical charge. He had a migraine he couldn't get rid of, and he was long overdue for some physical relief. Her scent, the softness of her skin, and her sensual voice were etched in his brain, and it was driving him crazy. He had no doubt that Elizabeth would welcome him into her bed, but after she displayed a hint of jealousy at the party, he decided to put the brakes on their relationship to slow things down.

It was Sunday, and while he tried his best not to work on the Lord's Day, sometimes he couldn't get out of it. He had attended the eight o'clock service at his church, and had a hard time getting away after being cornered by several single ladies in the congregation.

After pulling into the parking garage, he dialed Mason's cell number and waited for an answer. After the fourth ring, it went into voice mail, so he dialed again. This time, Mason picked up on the third ring.

"Hello?"

"Hey, bro. I was calling to see if Sunday dinner was on as usual."

Mason let out a breath and said, "I don't know. It's not a good time right now. Let me call you back."

Vincent shut his car off and said, "What's wrong? You don't sound too good. Is everything okay?"

"Nah, everything's not okay."

"Do you want to talk about it?" Vincent asked.

"Not right now, bro."

"Okay, but if you need me, I'm at the office."

"Cool," Mason replied before quickly hanging up the telephone.

Mason stepped out of his vehicle at the hotel whose name was printed on the key card in the gift. He walked over to the reception desk and showed his badge.

"Excuse me, sir, but I need to know what room goes with this card."

The desk clerk took the card key and ran it through a machine and said, "It goes to room eight-oh-three."

Mason smiled and said, "Thank you."

He went directly to the elevator and pushed the button for the eighth floor. When he stepped out of the elevator, he made his way down the hallway to room 803 and knocked. Seconds later, the door opened and he came face to face with the one woman he never thought he would see again. She was as beautiful as ever as she stood before him, scantily clad in a black lace panty and bra ensemble.

"What took you so long?" she asked with a huge smile on her face.

Mason's suspicions had now become a reality. The woman he thought he would never see again was back, but why?

"What the hell are you doing here, Lillian?"

Lillian was the assistant district attorney that Mason had a serious affair with a few years earlier. She was also the woman Cherise had run out of town when she threatened her with a gun after finding out about the affair.

Lillian smiled and pulled him inside her room. She immediately wrapped her arms around his neck and kissed him. Mason tried to remove her arms, but she had a tight grip on him.

"Oh my God! You still feel and taste so good."

Mason yanked her arms away from his neck and asked, "What's going on? Why are you sending me text messages and that crazy-ass gift?"

She made her way over to the bed and seductively crossed her legs. "Isn't it obvious, babe? I thought you would be happy to see me. I want you back, Mason. I've been miserable without you."

Mason stood in the middle of the hotel room and stared at her. She was still very beautiful, and he had to admit that seeing her aroused him.

"It's not going to happen, Lillian."

She stood and walked over to him and boldly caressed his crotch.

"You might not have a choice."

Vincent arrived at his office around ten o'clock. He didn't like coming into the office on Sundays, but sometimes it couldn't be helped. He didn't plan on staying long; he just wanted to finish up some paperwork before dinner at the Jernigans'. As he scanned through the stack of folders on his desk, his thoughts wandered back to his short conversation with Mason. There was tension in his voice, and his brother never showed stress unless it had something to do with Cherise or the family. Mason said he would call him back. He'd give him another hour. If he didn't hear from him by then, he would call Mason.

"Commander McKenzie," one of his officers said as he stepped inside his office. "You have a visitor."

"Visitor?" he asked as he stood and made his way over to the door. He wasn't expecting anyone, so it was a surprise when Elizabeth met him at the door.

"Good morning, Vincent. I hope I didn't catch you at a bad time?" she asked. "I brought a peace offering."

After thanking his officer for escorting Elizabeth to his office, he smiled at her and opened the box, which had a delicious strawberry cake inside.

"It looks delicious. Come on in and have a seat."

Vincent closed the door and set the cake on his desk and asked, "Did you bake this cake this morning?"

"Last night," she answered as she crossed her shapely legs.

Vincent's eyes couldn't help but admire them and her fabulous body in the burgundy suit she wore.

"You look beautiful."

"Thank you. I don't want to disturb you, but I came out here to apologize again for what I said at the party last night."

He waved her off and said, "Forget about it. We're on the same page now, right?"

"Yes, but you make it hard on a girl," she answered. "You're quite irresistible, Vincent."

"I wouldn't say that," he replied, trying not to blush. "Do you have any plans for dinner?"

"No."

"How would you like to have dinner with me and my family today? It'll give you a chance to get to know them a little better."

"I'd love to," she answered.

He looked at his watch and said, "I'll pick you up in about an hour or so."

She stood and said, "Great. Just call me when you're on the way."

He took her by the arm and walked her to the door and then gave her a soft kiss on the lips. "I will. Drive safely."

Vincent watched as Elizabeth walked down the hallway and onto the elevator. He sat down in his chair and thought about the possibilities with Elizabeth. Maybe he'd been too hard on her after all. She seemed genuinely apologetic, and she was extremely sexy. Bedding her might just be what he needed to get his mind and body off Cherise and on with his life.

Later that afternoon, Cherise moved around her mother's kitchen, helping with dinner. She had tried to call Mason to let him know she was at her parents' house, but got his voice-mail instead. It had been an exhausting morning, and now all she wanted to do was have a relaxing evening with her family. She had no idea where Mason was, but if she had to guess, she assumed he was somewhere investigating whoever sent him the erotic gift.

Janelle walked into the kitchen and asked, "Can't I help?"

"Sure you can," she replied as she hugged her daughter. Cherise tilted Janelle's chin upward and stared down in eyes that were exactly like hers. As she looked, she saw something else very familiar to her—undeniable love.

Cherise pulled the bar stool over to the kitchen counter so Janelle could finish making the salad that was going to go with the pork chops and cheesy potatoes.

"Is this good, Momma?" Janelle asked as she topped the salad with crunchy croutons.

Cherise glanced over at the bowl and said, "It's perfect. You can go ahead and get the salad dressing out and take it into the dining room."

Janelle hopped off the bar stool and opened the refrigerator. After putting the bottles of salad dressing on the table, she ran out into the hallway and yelled, "Uncle Vincent's here!"

Cherise could hear her parents greeting Vincent, and then she heard another voice, a female voice.

"Welcome to our home," Patricia said to Elizabeth.

"Thank you," Elizabeth replied shyly.

"Make yourself at home," Jonathan said as he made his way back out into the backyard.

Vincent hung her jacket in the closet alongside his. He turned back to Patricia and gave her a kiss on the cheek. Patricia escorted the couple to the family room, where they found Mase and Janelle playing a video game.

"Hey, Unc," Mase greeted him without taking his eyes off the TV screen.

He patted his nephew on the shoulders and said, "Hey, nephew. Janelle, may I have a kiss?"

Janelle put the game on pause and jumped into her uncle's arms. She gave him a kiss and asked, "Who is she?"

He sat her on the floor and said, "This is my friend, Elizabeth. Elizabeth, this is my niece, Janelle, and my nephew, Mason Jr."

Elizabeth held her hand out to them and said, "It's nice to meet you."

Mase quickly shook her hand, but Janelle just stared at her.

"Janelle, shake Elizabeth's hand."

She shook Elizabeth's hand and then went back to playing the game with her brother.

Vincent sat down on the sofa and asked, "Where's Mason and C. J.?"

"I'm not sure where Mason is, but Cherise is in the kitchen," Patricia replied. "Elizabeth, would you like some tea or lemonade while you wait for dinner?"

"Lemonade will be fine. Thank you."

"I'll get it." Vincent stood and made his way into the kitchen with Patricia, where he found Cherise putting the pork chops on a tray.

She glanced up at Vincent and said, "Hey."

He took a glass out of the cabinet and then opened the refrigerator. "Hey, C. J. You have it smelling good in here."

"She cooked the entire dinner herself," Patricia announced proudly. "All I did was bake the rolls."

"Was that Elizabeth's voice I heard?" she asked.

"Yeah. I hope you don't mind that I invited her over," he replied as he poured lemonade.

Cherise removed the large casserole dish of cheesy potatoes from the oven and said, "Of course not. Why wouldn't you bring your girlfriend over?"

He laughed out loud. "There you go. Don't start that again."

"You two are funny," Patricia said before walking out into the backyard to take Jonathan more pork chops for the grill. Vincent walked closer to Cherise and asked, "Where's Mason? I talked to him earlier and he sounded a little tense."

"I don't know where he is," she answered as she removed her oven mitts. "He left the house a couple of hours ago. I haven't heard from him since."

"Is something wrong?"

"I don't want to talk about it, Vincent," she answered before walking out of the kitchen so she could greet Elizabeth.

Mason stared at the picture of the little girl. He mumbled, "I can't believe this. Are you serious?"

"Of course I'm serious," Lillian replied as she caressed his shoulders.

"Why are you just now telling me?" he asked.

"Would it have made a difference if I had told you sooner?"

He put his head in his hands and said, "Of course it would have, Lillian."

"I'm sorry I didn't tell you, baby, but I had my reasons. I know you still have feelings for me. You proved that to me over and over again. What we have is indescribable and you know it. If it wasn't for the fact that your wife shoved that gun in my face, I would've stayed and fought for you, but I'm no fool. I wasn't going to stay here and let her kill me, our child, and my career, so I packed my bags and rolled out. I was hoping that you would've joined me in D.C., but you made your choice. I'm only here because I need to know if you still love me and want to be with me and our daughter."

He looked over at her and asked, "Have you forgotten that I'm married?"

"No, Mason, I haven't forgotten, but you never seemed concerned about it when you were in my bed night after night."

Mason sighed because Lillian was right. When he had an affair with her, he forgot about everything and everybody, except her. She was every man's dream, who was at his beck and call any time he wanted her.

"Are you sure I'm the father?"

Lillian frowned and said, "Of course I am. I wasn't sleeping with anybody else. You know I wouldn't lie about this."

"Do you have any idea what this is going to do to my family?"

"What about us? We deserve to have you in our lives too. I didn't create her all by myself, Mason."

Still in shock over the news, he said, "I know you didn't. Look, I'm sorry, and I have to admit that I don't know what to say right now. You can't expect me to just leave my family over this. I care about you, but my family means everything to me. I need time to think."

Lillian lowered her head and said, "I didn't come here to make you angry, Mason. Nothing's changed as far as I'm concerned. I'm still just as in love with you now as I was then."

"How old is she?" he softly asked.

"She's nine, almost ten."

"Nine?" he repeated. "I still can't believe you never thought it was important to tell me."

"It crossed my mind a few times, but I changed my mind, since it was obvious you didn't want to be with me anymore."

"Why now? After all these years, why are you here telling me about her now?"

"She's sick, and I was hoping you would want to be her father now."

Hearing that the little girl staring back at him was sick concerned him. While he didn't have a relationship with her, she was his blood, and he didn't want any harm to come to her.

"What do you mean, sick? What's wrong with her?"

"She has juvenile diabetes, and she needs a kidney transplant. I was hoping that maybe you could have your son or daughter tested to see if they could donate one of theirs."

Mason nearly blacked out. It was going from bad to worse in record time. While he felt bad for the child, there was no way in hell he could do what she was requesting. Cherise would never allow it anyway, and he could never explain something like this to his children.

"Now I know you're crazy," Mason replied. "I have to go," he said as he set the child's picture on the bed and headed toward the door.

"Where are you going?" she asked as she blocked his path to the door.

He put his hands on her shoulders and scooted her out of his way.

"I said I need time to think," he replied. "Don't call or send me any more text messages. I'll contact you after I sort all this out."

She wrapped her arms around his waist and kissed him on the lips. "Don't you want to know your daughter's name?"

Mason paused and asked, "Sure, Lillian. What's her name?"

"Her name is McKenzie."

He laughed. "I can't believe you. Just place a billboard on the child's forehead."

She rubbed her body against his and said, "I figured if I named her McKenzie she would have your name, even if we never ended up together."

"Good-bye, Lillian," he replied as he opened the door.

"Don't keep me waiting too long. This is serious, Mason."

He stopped halfway down the hallway and asked, "How long will you be in town?"

"As long as I have to be, baby."

"I'll be in touch," he replied as he turned and walked away.

Mason climbed into his car and leaned against his steering wheel. He felt sick to his stomach. It was bad enough that Lillian was back, but the announcement of a child made things a lot more complicated.

He started the ignition and pulled out of the parking lot, not sure if he should join his family at his in-laws' or not. If he didn't go, Cherise would probably wonder what he was up to. If he did go, he would have to put on an award-winning performance because his mind was definitely preoccupied with Lillian and everything she revealed to him.

Chapter Nine

Mason arrived at the Jernigans' house and walked inside. After greeting everyone including Cherise, he motioned for Vincent to join him in the backyard.

"What's up? Why didn't you call me back?"

"I was following up on some leads," he explained.

"What kind of leads?" Vincent asked.

Mason looked over his shoulders to make sure no one could hear them.

"I'm in trouble, bro. Lillian's back in town."

"The D.A. Lillian?" Vincent asked. "I thought she moved to D.C."

"She did, but she's back, and she's been sending me all sorts of crazy text messages. She even sent a sex gift to the house for my birthday. Cherise saw it and went ballistic. Now she thinks I'm having an affair. Then to top things off, Lillian's claiming I'm the father of her nine-year-old daughter."

"A daughter? Is it true?" Vincent asked.

"She looks just like me, and get this . . . she's sick. She has juvenile diabetes and needs a kidney transplant."

Patricia stuck her head out the door, interrupting them. "You two come on inside so we can eat."

"We're coming, Patricia," Vincent replied before turning back to his brother. "Pull yourself together, Mason. I don't care what that woman told you. You need to get a DNA test before you go any further. We'll talk about this later."

***

Elizabeth seemed to enjoy herself at dinner. Janelle eventually warmed up to her, and even helped her cut slices of her strawberry cake for the family. Cherise and Mason were noticeably quiet, and while Vincent had an insight on Mason's detachment from family conversation, he didn't know what was going on with Cherise. He first thought it was because he brought Elizabeth to dinner. Then he thought maybe Cherise knew about Lillian and her child.

"So, Elizabeth, Vincent tells us you were an accountant," Patricia stated.

"Yes, ma'am. I work for an agency in Buckhead."

"Are you from the Atlanta area?"

"No, ma'am. I'm originally from Columbia, South Carolina. I went to college at Spelman and fell in love with Atlanta, so I decided to make it my home."

"Good choice," Jonathan chimed in. "Do you have any other siblings?"

"Yes, sir, I have a younger brother in the military, and a sister who's in college at North Carolina A and T."

"What about your parents?" Patricia asked.

Vincent laughed. If Elizabeth was feeling pressured by all their questions, he had to admit she was holding her own pretty well.

"Hey, guys, give Elizabeth a break. I'm sure you can give her the Perry Mason treatment the next time she comes over."

"It's okay, Vincent. I don't mind," she said before turning her attention back to Patricia. "My parents still live in South Carolina. My dad works at an assembly plant, and my mother is an elementary school teacher."

Patricia smiled and then said, "Well, we'd love to meet them if they come to Atlanta any time soon."

"Yes, ma'am."

Patricia turned her attention to Mason and Cherise. "Why are you two so quiet? Are you still tired from the party last night?"

Cherise picked up her plate and stood. "Something like that, Momma. Is anyone else finished with their dessert plate?"

Vincent and Mase handed her their empty plates, but when she looked over at Mason, he hadn't even touched his cake.

"I'm full from dinner. I'm going to take mine home and eat it later," he said to her.

Cherise stared at him for a moment and then said, "Kids, get your things so we can go home."

"Why are you leaving so early?" Jonathan asked.

"I have to go to work early in the morning, Daddy, and I'll probably have to do a double shift. I want to get home and relax."

"What about you, Mason? Are you going to hang out with us for a while?"

Mason stood and picked up his dessert plate. "I can't stay long, but I can help you guys clean up before I roll out. I have to work in the morning too."

Patricia looked over at Vincent and Elizabeth. "Well, that leaves you guys. We'd love for you to stay for a while, but if you have something else to do, we understand."

Vincent put his arm around Elizabeth's shoulders and said, "We can stay a little while longer if it's okay with Elizabeth."

She nodded in agreement. Jonathan wiped his mouth with his napkin and said, "Good. I'll make some coffee."

***

Cherise made her way into the kitchen, where she loaded the dishwasher. Mason followed her into the kitchen so he could wrap up his slice of cake.

She turned to him and asked, "Where have you been for the last few hours?"

"Trying to find out who sent me that gift," he replied as he wrapped his cake in Saran Wrap.

She folded her arms and asked, "Well, did you find out who sent it?"

Without making eye contact, he said, "I'm still working things out. I'll let you know when I have some answers."

Cherise studied his body language and sensed that he was hiding something from her, but decided not to push the issue.

"I'm getting ready to take the kids home. Are you coming?" she asked.

"I'll be there shortly," he answered before walking out of the kitchen and into the family room.

Thirty minutes later, Cherise and the kids left. Vincent, Mason, and Elizabeth relaxed out on the patio with Jonathan and Patricia for the next hour and a half. Vincent noticed how Mason kept looking at his watch, and decided to cut the evening short. His brother was in distress and he needed his help.

After thanking the Jernigans for another enjoyable Sunday, Vincent and Elizabeth walked out to his car.

"Elizabeth, do me a favor and take my car home. I have to talk to Mason, and it'll probably take a while. I'll get him to bring me by later to pick it up."

She took the keys out of his hands and said, "Are you sure?"

He smiled and opened the driver's side door for her. "I'm sure. I'll call when we're on the way. Drive safely."

"I will," she answered before starting the car and pulling away.

Mason came out of the house and met Vincent in the driveway. "You let her drive your car?"

"Yeah, and if she totals it, you're paying for it," Vincent joked. "Let's go so we can talk."

Vincent and Mason waved to Jonathan and Patricia as they climbed into Mason's car and disappeared down the street.

Lillian paced the floor of her hotel room. Mason said he would contact her, but after seeing him, she could hardly wait to find out what he was going to do about her and their child.

"Come on, Mason, call me," she mumbled to herself.

She looked at the clock and watched it go from two o'clock to eight o'clock, and still no call from Mason. She sent him a text, but received no response. She dialed his number and it went into voicemail. That's when she decided to get dressed and take a drive by his house. If he was trying to ignore her, it wasn't going to work.

In the backyard, Cherise soaked her tense muscles in the hot tub. It had been a long, stressful day, and the hot bubbles dancing around her soothed her body. As she sat there with her eyes closed, she felt herself starting to doze off.

"Crazy day, huh?" Mason asked, startling her out of her sleep.

Cherise quickly sat up, splashing water, and said, "You scared me, Mason. I didn't hear you come in."

He walked closer to her and said, "I didn't want to disturb you. You looked so peaceful."

"I thought you said you were coming home right behind me."

"I'm sorry. I had some things to take care of," he replied as he caressed her lovely face.

Cherise looked down at his other hand and asked, "What's in the bag?"

He chuckled and said, "Janelle called and asked me to bring her some ice cream."

"That little con artist," Cherise joked. "She's had enough sweets today."

"Let her have a small bowl. She knows I can't say no to her," he revealed. "Listen, after I look in on the kids, would you like some company?"

She stood and grabbed a nearby towel. "It's late, and I was just about to get out. Maybe some other time. I'm going inside to take a shower."

"That's a date," he replied as he turned off the jets and helped her out of the hot tub. After handing her the bag with the ice cream, he asked her to take it inside so he could put the cover over the hot tub.

Seconds later, Mason noticed the headlights of a car in the driveway. He walked to the gate and watched as Lillian climbed out of the car. Startled by her boldness, he bolted out of the gate and grabbed her before she could get to the porch.

"What the hell are you doing here?" he asked angrily.

"You said you would call me," she replied. "Why haven't you called?"

"I didn't mean today," he said as he opened her car door and forced her back inside the car.

"When are you going to talk to me, Mason? I need to know what you're going to do."

He pointed his finger in her face and said, "I told you I needed time to think. Don't you ever come to my house again. If you do, you can forget about me or my help."

"You would do that to your daughter?" she asked.

"This is my family you're messing with. Just go back to the hotel and wait for me to contact you," he said before walking back into the backyard.

Lillian angrily drove off, while Mason made his way up to the bedroom. By the grace of God, Cherise was still in the shower, preventing her from seeing his altercation with Lillian in the driveway.

Across town, Vincent sat in Elizabeth's living room after Mason dropped him off to get his car. He called on the way over, which gave her time to take a quick shower and to change the linens on her bed, just in case. She was a little nervous, but hoped that tonight would be the beginning of many nights. She wanted their first night together to be perfect, so she lit several scented candles and then smoothed down her short pink nightgown before rejoining him.

"Wow! What did I do to deserve this?" he asked.

"I take it that you like it," she said as she twirled around to give him a three hundred and sixty degree view.

"I would have to be blind not to," he replied as he pulled her into his arms and kissed her lovingly on the lips. As he kissed her, he remembered that he told her he wanted to slow things down, but he hadn't expected her to make this kind of move on him. He was a man, and he recognized a sexy woman when he saw one. Her mouth was sweet, and her body was soft, igniting his body.

He made eye contact with her before his hands slowly moved down her backside and under her nightgown, until he had her soft, firm bottom in his hands. Elizabeth closed her eyes and panted as he gently kissed her neck and soft lips. She was melting right before his eyes, and was becoming weak in the knees as he continued to devour her lips.

Breathless, she broke their kiss and slowly led him into her bedroom and began to seductively undress him. Vincent let her do her thang, and within seconds, she had him completely bare. She was in awe of his magnificent body as her hands explored every muscle. He tilted her chin upwards and smiled as their eyes made contact. He pulled her nightgown over her head and tossed it on the floor.

Elizabeth scooted back on the bed, allowing him access to her curvy body. He ran his tongue over her ample breasts. Using a condom for protection, he slowly entered her body. Elizabeth gasped and bit down on her lower lip before experiencing the best loving she'd ever had.

Vincent tossed and flipped Elizabeth around so many ways her head was spinning. He appreciated the fact that she was doing everything within her power to please him, and she was good, but she wasn't able to compete with Cherise. In fact, no woman could; but tonight, Elizabeth was able to quench his thirst for Cherise on all levels. It was a huge milestone for them, and while she was the one who initiated the booty call, he had to guard his heart and make sure she knew he still wanted to take their relationship slow.

At four A.M., Vincent sat up on the side of Elizabeth's bed and started getting dressed. She rolled over and whispered, "Why are you leaving so early?"

"I wish I could stay, but I have a lot to do today," he replied as he cupped her face and gave her a kiss on the lips. "You're a wonderful woman, Elizabeth."

She blushed and said, "I hope you enjoyed last night as much as I did."

"Oh, I definitely enjoyed it," he replied as he slipped into his shoes. "I thought you could tell that already."

Elizabeth wrapped her arms around his neck and said, "I wasn't sure. When can I see you again?"

"Soon," he answered as he nibbled on her ear. "Get some sleep. I'll give you a call later today."

Chapter Ten

Cherise was running late to work, and when she stepped outside her house, she froze. All four tires on her SUV were slashed, causing her to get an instant migraine.

"Damn it!" she screamed before dialing Mason's cell number. He was still inside the house getting dressed, and so were the kids.

Mase stepped out on the porch and asked, "What's wrong, Momma?"

She hung up her cell phone and said, "Tell your father to get out here now. I have a flat."

Mase yelled for his father before running down the stairs to inspect the tires alongside his mother.

"All four of your tires are flat, Momma."

Cherise put her arm around her son's neck and said, "I know, baby. This is going to cost me a fortune."

"Why would someone cut your tires?" he asked.

"People do all kinds of evil things for no reason, son. Go back in the house and make sure your sister is ready," she said as she handed him her briefcase. "I'm going to have to get my truck towed to the shop, and your father is going to have to take you guys to school."

Mason exited the house, buttoning up his shirt. "What's up, babe?"

She pointed to her tires and said, "You tell me."

Mason put his hands on his head in disbelief. Could Lillian have been so stupid as to cut his wife's tires? He knew she was angry, but to damage Cherise's vehicle didn't do anything but hurt the situation.

"Do you think that woman did this?" Cherise asked.

Mason cursed before kneeling down to inspect the tires. "I don't know what to think. Why didn't you pull into the garage last night?"

"Oh! You're making this out to be my fault?" she asked. "I didn't think it was mandatory that I parked in the garage every night."

"I didn't mean it like that, sweetheart," Mason replied in defense. "I was just asking a question."

"I know, and I'm sorry," she apologized. "Will you be able to stay here and wait on the tow truck? I really need to get to the office."

He looked at his watch and said, "I can't. I have to be in court in two hours."

Frustrated, she asked, "Well, can you at least take the kids to school?"

"Yes, but they're going to have to hustle," he replied as he headed back up the stairs. "I'll call the towing service for you. Do you think your dad can run you to work?"

She followed him up the stairs and back into the house. "I'm not going to bother them. I'll just catch a cab."

Mason yelled up the stairs for the kids before putting his wallet in his back pocket and picking up his keys.

"I'm sorry, honey. If I didn't have to be in court, I could stay."

She waved him off and said, "Don't worry about it. Just go."

Cherise set her purse down on the table in the hallway as the kids ran down the steps to give her a hug.

"Have a good day at school, guys."

"Good-bye, Momma," Janelle said as she hugged her mother's waist.

"Bye, baby."

Mase gave her a kiss on the cheek and said, "I love you, Momma."

"I love you too, son. Go ahead so you won't be late."

Cherise watched as Janelle and Mase climbed inside their father's car. Before walking out the door, Mason turned to Cherise and said, "I'm sorry about this, sweetheart. Call or text me after the tow truck comes."

She grabbed his arm, stopping him from walking away.

"Mason, if that woman did this to my car, it means she'll probably do anything. I don't want my children caught up in this, so you'd better find out who did this before I do; because if I find her first, it's not going to be pretty."

He hugged her and said, "Don't worry, Cherise. I got this."

An hour and a half later, Cherise was able to catch a cab and meet her team where a body had been found by boaters floating just off the banks of the Chattahoochee River. It was going to take several hours to process the crime scene, giving the tire shop ample time to replace her damaged tires.

After court, Mason decided to catch a bite and call Lillian before he returned to his office. When he dialed her number, she immediately answered.

"It's about time."

Mason paced outside the deli. "Did you cut my wife's tires last night?"

"Aren't you going to say hello first?" she casually asked.

"I don't have time for that. Did you cut her tires?"

She hesitated for a moment and then said, "I had to do something to get your attention."

Mason angrily hung up the phone and nearly ran over to Lillian's hotel room. When he got to the door this time, he didn't knock. Instead, he used the key card and let himself in.

Lillian had no idea he was in the room until he yanked open the shower curtain and pulled her body out of the shower. He covered her mouth with his hand to keep her from screaming, and threw her wet, sudsy body on the bed. She was startled at first, but when she realized it was the love of her life straddling her body, she relaxed.

"Stop fighting me, Lillian," he demanded as he pointed his finger in her face.

"I know what you want," she replied as she wiggled underneath him and ran her hands over his backside.

"I'm not kidding, Lillian. I want you to stay away from my wife. That shit you did is costing me money."

She laughed mischievously and said, "Give me some and I'll never go near her again."

He climbed off her and took a few steps backward. "You've got to be crazy. It's over between us."

She walked over to him and rubbed her wet body against his. "Is it?" she asked just before she unzipped his pants, dropped to her knees, and engulfed him. Mason was immediately paralyzed in ecstasy as she skillfully pleasured him.

"Lillian," he moaned softly as he grabbed her hair with both fists, guiding her. The last thing she needed was guidance. She smiled up at him as she increased her motion, and then slowly pulled back. She did this over and over again, until she had him cursing and nearly in tears. Mason felt his body spasm as he peaked and let out a loud grunt, signaling his release.

Lillian continued her sensual assault, but in a slower pace. He was almost where she wanted him, so she stopped, only to lead him back over to the bed. As she lay before him spread eagle on the comforter, she whispered, "I got you all ready for me now. Come on, baby."

"Damn you, Lillian," he replied as he swung the door open and sprinted down the hallway, zipping up his pants along the way. When he arrived at the elevator, he frantically pushed the button so he could escape. He could hear her laughter echoing down the hallway as she called out to him.

The elevator door finally opened and he dove inside and pushed the button for the lobby. When he stepped into the lobby, he immediately became nauseated, so he ran to the nearest men's room and threw up. He finally made his way over to the sink and stared at himself in the mirror. He doused his face with cold water and wondered how he had let Lillian get to him. It was unthinkable, but he knew why. She was like a witch, and he knew he had a weakness around her, so he had to make sure he didn't allow himself to come in contact with her ever again.

Just then, his cell phone rang, and as expected, it was Lillian.

He answered and said, "Don't call me anymore!"

She giggled as she pulled the sheet over her large breasts. "You know you don't mean that. I know you, Mason McKenzie, and you loved what I just did to you."

"Go to hell!"

"Baby, I know how you smell, taste, and feel, and I know exactly what you like. There's no way your wifey can do you like I can."

"Leave my wife out of this," he replied as he made his way out of the restroom and onto the sidewalk.

"Sweetheart, your wife is all up in this, so don't get it twisted."

Mason tried to calm himself, but he was unsuccessful. "No! Don't *you* get it twisted! Lose my number, Lillian! I mean it when I say don't call me again."

"Don't call you? Please! You can't resist me any more than I can resist you. We were made from the same mold, Mason, and we will be together whether you want to believe it or not."

Mason climbed into his car and said, "Go back to D.C., Lillian. Until I have the DNA test results in my hands, we have nothing more to discuss."

She jumped out of the bed and said, "I love you, Mason."

Angry, he hung up the phone and threw it on the floorboard of the car and sped off down the street.

As soon as Mason walked through his door, Vincent knew that whatever reason he was there, it wasn't going to be good.

"You look like hell, bro. What's up?" Vincent asked.

Mason closed Vincent's door and sat down in the chair across from him. He put his hands over his face. "I put another nail in my coffin this morning."

Vincent got up from his desk, poured Mason a cup of coffee, and handed it to him before sitting back down. "What did you do?" Vincent asked.

"Lillian showed up at the house last night."

"Are you serious?" Vincent asked. "Where was C. J.?"

"In the shower," he answered. "Cherise doesn't know Lillian's in town, and I'm not telling her."

Vincent put his hand on Mason's shoulder and said, "You have a stalker, bro."

"That's only half of it. Lillian's out of control, bro. She slit the tires on Cherise's truck, too. I had to go set things straight with her."

Vincent closed his eyes briefly and hoped his brother didn't harm Lillian.

"What did you do?" Vincent asked.

"Nothing much. I just manhandled her a little bit."

"What do you mean?" Vincent asked curiously.

Mason looked up at his brother and said, "I was pissed; so pissed that I let myself into her room and yanked her ass out of the shower and threw her on the bed."

"You know this could've turned out bad, don't you? She could have you arrested for breaking and entering."

Mason laughed and said, "The hell she can. She's the one who gave me the key. I'm her boo, remember?"

Vincent twirled around in his chair and said, "That's not funny, Mason. Is she going to chill or what?"

Mason quickly stood and walked across the room. He leaned against the wall. "I don't know what she's going to do. She has this fantasy about us being together, but I told her to leave town until I can figure this out."

"She sounds obsessed. You'd better watch your back with this one, and you better hope she don't pay C. J. a visit."

Mason got angry all over again. The thought of Lillian talking to Cherise angered him, and the fact that she had shown up at their house made it even more of a possibility.

"I'd kill her myself if she tried that bullshit again."

"She's a woman, bro, and she seems determined to get you back by your own doing—or by default—by breaking up your marriage. Either way, you're a fool if you let this happen."

"I hear everything you're saying, Vincent, but there's something inside of me that wants her, even though Cherise is my heart."

"It's only because you've been there before and you know what she's like. Instead of reminiscing on your love affair with her, you should recall the hurt, shame, and pain your affair put on C. J. She could've killed that woman, and I have no doubt she wanted to. She has a temper, but she loves you and your children more. Killing Lillian wasn't worth her risking her family."

Mason covered his face and said, "I hear every word you're saying, and you're right, but I still can't explain it. One minute she was making me so angry that I wanted to squeeze the life out of her; the next minute she was on her knees doing what she does best, and I loved every second of it."

Vincent shook his head in disbelief. Had anything he said sunk into Mason's distorted brain at all? Maybe he did have some type of sickness instead of a weakness when it came to women.

"Mason! Have you listened to a word I've said? After all you've been through with C. J.—the promises, the heartache, and rebuilding of trust—you're going to throw it all out the window in one afternoon?"

"It's not like that," Mason replied. "I didn't go there for that, but at that moment, she had me."

Vincent cut him off and slammed his fist down on the desk. "Did you sleep with her?"

Mason lowered his head and whispered, "No, but a part of me really, really wanted to."

"I don't know what to say to you anymore, Mason. A piece of wild ass versus a beautiful, loving wife makes it a no-brainer."

"I wish I could explain it to you, bro, but I can't. I love my wife, but Lillian is an important part of my life too," Mason admitted in defense. "I never expected her to come back to

Atlanta and drop a child in my lap, but we have a past together, and the possibility is there, so I have to go through the
motions until I know the truth."

"Are you in love with her, or is it the sex?" Vincent asked
curiously.

Mason thought about Vincent's question for a long thirty
seconds and then said, "I think it's just the sex, but I do have
feelings for her. You know I love Cherise, but Lillian is actually cool."

"Do you really know how to love your wife? I'm only asking
because I'm trying to understand why you would get intimate
with a woman who could put an end to your marriage."

Mason stared at his brother for a moment and then admitted, "All I know is that Lillian is exciting, beautiful, sexy, and
crazy all rolled into one. She makes me lose touch with reality
and everything else."

"So, you're basically asking your wife for a divorce?"

"Of course not."

"That's what you're doing, and I don't think you see it.
Get your goddamn life together and stop taking your wife for
granted. It's going to be hard for her to forgive you again."

Mason stood and said, "I forgave you."

Vincent smiled. He knew that one day Mason would use
an opportunity to remind him about his affair with Cherise.
He stood and walked over to his brother until they were eye
to eye.

Vincent pointed his finger in Mason's face and said, "I appreciate you forgiving me for what I did with Cherise, but I
loved her during the time you didn't give a damn about her
or your son. That woman was broken beyond broken, and I
was pissed. You wouldn't listen to me when I was trying to
tell you there was a problem. As usual, you refused to believe

there was a problem, and continued to work for weeks at a time, while rolling around with those whores.

"You weren't home to see her crying her eyes out after finding lipstick stains on your briefs. You weren't there when she took telephone calls from women telling her they'd slept with you. And you weren't there when she started drinking to get rid of the pain and the feeling of abandonment. She could've lost her job, Mason."

Mason said, "I know I made mistakes with my wife."

"Do you, Mason?" Vincent asked. "I didn't plan on having an affair with C. J., but I was there in some of the darkest times of her life. You were the one who made the decisions that kept you away for weeks, not me, and you know what the sad thing was? When you did come home, you acted like a stranger and didn't want to have anything to do with her.

"There was even a point when I thought she might harm herself. I'm sorry I betrayed you, because you're my brother, but you were an arrogant, self centered, uncaring asshole back then, and you're about to do it all over again."

Mason scratched his head as Vincent's words sunk in. He loved his brother and knew he would never vindictively take advantage of his wife or family. The damage to his marriage was by his own hands, but it didn't change the fact that it did happen, and he was still a little haunted by it.

"Listen, Vincent, I'd be lying if I said I wasn't still a little paranoid about your relationship with Cherise. All I'm asking is for a little understanding over this thing with Lillian. You know what it's like to love someone you know you could never have. Give me time to figure this out with Lillian, and once I know if her child is mine, I'll know where to go from here."

"Whatever you say, bro," Vincent replied as he turned toward his desk.

Mason grabbed him by the arm, stopping him. "Vincent, I want you to know that while I'm still having issues about you and Cherise, I really have forgiven you. I realize if it hadn't been you, it could've been someone else who could've really hurt her or my son."

"I would've never let that happen," Vincent replied as he sat down. "Get out of here so you can go clear up this mess with Lillian—and try to keep your hands to yourself."

Mason thanked his brother and then left the office in a daze. His heart was pounding in his chest. He had no idea how Cherise would take the news if she found out Lillian was behind the text messages, cutting her tires, the gift, and a possible illegitimate child.

Chapter Eleven

A couple of weeks had passed, and luckily for Mason, there were no more text messages or signs of Lillian. He prayed she had taken his advice and returned to D.C. and given him time to think about the situation. He had to resolve the issue regarding the possibility of a daughter, so a trip to D.C. was necessary to put the matter to rest once and for all.

A few nights later, Mason arrived home earlier than normal, just as Cherise was headed back out the door to work a second shift. He removed his jacket and then put his gun and holster on top of the refrigerator before greeting her with a kiss.

"Hey, babe."

"Hey, sweetheart. Listen, we're really busy down at the office, so I don't know when I'll be home. Dinner's ready, and the kids are upstairs doing their homework. I have to run. I'm late."

He tore off a piece of catfish and put it in his mouth. "This is delicious."

"Daddy went fishing this morning. He dropped it off this evening," she replied before giving him a quick kiss on the lips. "Call me if you need to get a hold of me."

He grabbed her around the waist and held her in his arms

as he seductively said, "I'd like to get a hold of you right now."

"I'm sure you would, but I can't. I have to get to work. I'll take a rain check though."

Mason playfully patted her on the backside before releasing her. "That's a date."

Cherise picked up her purse as Mason opened the garage door. "Drive carefully. The rain is starting to pick up."

"I will," she replied as she climbed inside her truck and drove off to yet another crime scene near the Chattahoochee River. This time, it was an execution-style shooting with similarities to the previous murder. The only difference was that this body wasn't placed in the river, but it was near it. Maybe the perpetrator was interrupted before he or she could finish dumping the body. In any case, Cherise was going to have to spend time out in the rain on the wet, muddy banks of the river.

Vincent and Elizabeth sat in his loft in front of a warm fireplace, sipping Merlot. It wasn't his favorite flavor of wine, but it would do. Tonight she had insisted on cooking dinner for him at his loft, and he accepted. She had excellent culinary skills, and she wanted to try a new shrimp pasta dish that she had found on the Food Network.

He hadn't seen Elizabeth since their romp in bed, but he'd spoken with her each day. Their relationship was going well, but he still wanted to take things slow. In fact, he had gone out on dates with a couple of other women he had dated in the past. Tonight, Elizabeth was hoping for another sensual encounter with the man who she was falling quickly in love with.

"Looks like we're out of wine," Vincent noted. "Would you like some more?"

"I'd love some," she replied as she curled her legs under her body on the sofa.

"I'm out, but my neighbor downstairs has somewhat of a wine closet, and we always hook each other up. I'll go down and get another bottle," he said as he grabbed his keys off the table.

"Are you sure it's okay? I don't want it to be an inconvenience."

He opened the door and said, "It's no inconvenience. Sit tight. I'll be right back."

Elizabeth smiled and took the last sip of wine before walking onto the balcony. As she looked out over the Atlanta skyline, her thoughts were interrupted when Vincent's telephone rang. She stepped back inside the loft and listened as the caller left a message:

"Vincent, it's Cherise. I hope you're home. I'm leaving a crime scene, and I'm wet, covered in mud, and I need to take a shower. Call me back so I'll know if it's okay to come over. I could also use a couple of hours of sleep, too, before going back to work. Call me back."

Elizabeth was hoping for an uninterrupted evening with Vincent. If Cherise came over, more than likely, the evening would end early, or be a threesome for the rest of the night. She'd seen how close Vincent was with his sister-in-law, and contrary to what he said, she believed there was more to their relationship. Taking a chance, she walked over to his answering machine, played back the message, erased it, and deleted the number from his caller ID. She knew what she did was wrong, but it was worth it to hopefully get some more loving from the man who in one night had turned her out and turned her world upside down.

Minutes later, Vincent walked back into the loft with two

bottles of wine in hand. One bottle was an expensive Chardonnay, and the other, a Zinfandel. He popped open the Zinfandel and refilled their glasses before sitting down. Elizabeth took a sip and then casually crawled over in his lap, straddling him.

"This is nice," he said with a smile as he caressed her back.

She gave him a long, loving kiss, and then whispered, "Why don't we take it to the bedroom?"

Vincent aggressively pulled her hips closer to him and asked, "What's wrong with right here?"

Elizabeth giggled and quickly started unbuttoning her blouse. Vincent admired her exhibition as he patiently watched her perform a strip tease in front of him. It was at that moment that he heard a noise coming from his front door. He jumped up, knocking Elizabeth to the ground, and ran over to the door, but he was too late. While Elizabeth scrambled to put her clothes on, Vincent intercepted the intruder.

"What are you doing here?" Vincent yelled at Cherise as she stepped inside the loft.

"Didn't you get my message?" she asked, clearly embarrassed.

"What message? I didn't get any message. When did you call?"

Cherise stood there, soaking wet and muddy, and noticed Elizabeth buttoning her blouse.

"I don't know, maybe thirty minutes ago," she revealed. "When you didn't call me back, I figured you weren't home. I'm sorry I let myself in. I can leave if you want me to," she answered as she opened the door to leave.

Vincent pushed the door closed and said, "It's okay. Besides, you're dripping all over my floor."

"Thank you," Cherise replied before looking over at Vincent's date. "Hi, Elizabeth, I'm sorry I interrupted—"

"It's okay, C. J. You didn't interrupt anything," Vincent replied, angering Elizabeth.

"I'll just go take my shower so I can get out of your way," Cherise stated before disappearing down the hallway.

Once she was gone, he looked over at Elizabeth and asked, "Did my phone ring while I was out?"

Lying, she said, "Not that I know of. I was out on the balcony for a few minutes, but I don't remember hearing it ring."

He thought to himself a minute as he looked for answers in her eyes. Cherise said she left a message, so even if Elizabeth didn't hear the phone, there should be a message on his answering machine. There wasn't. Maybe Cherise dialed the wrong number. There was no use trying to figure things out now. Cherise was there now, and it was only right for him to make sure she was comfortable before she had to go back to work.

"I'll be back in a sec," he told Elizabeth before walking toward the hallway. "I need to go check on C. J."

Elizabeth poured herself another glass of wine and breathed a sigh of relief before sitting back down on the sofa.

In the bathroom, Cherise stripped out of her wet clothes and put them in a plastic bag, but before she could get in the shower, Vincent knocked on the door.

"C. J., can I get you anything?"

"Yes, you can get me something to put on, and I need to throw these filthy clothes in the washer."

"Give them to me so I can go ahead and start the washer."

Cherise wrapped her body in a towel and then allowed him to enter the bathroom.

He walked in and immediately noticed her muscular legs.

The towel she had wasn't big enough to completely cover her body, so he was able to get a glimpse.

"You stink," he joked as he picked up the bag of dirty clothing.

"I've been in the Chattahoochee River. How do you expect me to smell?" she replied with a laugh.

"I got a text from my office about it. Do you think it's related to the other one?"

She tugged on the towel and said, "Looks like it."

"Keep me posted, but I bet it's drug related," he said as he turned to walk out.

"Vincent, before you leave, I want to tell you I really am sorry for busting in here on you and Elizabeth. I did leave you a message."

"I believe you," he answered with a smile. "I'll see if I can find you something to put on."

"Thank you. Is it okay if I catch a couple of hours of sleep before I go back to work?"

He smiled as he opened the bathroom door and said, "My casa, your casa."

"Will you also apologize to Elizabeth again for me?"

"Sure," he answered before walking out into the hallway.

Cherise closed the door and dropped her towel before stepping into the shower. The hot, sudsy water of the shower felt wonderful on her skin, and if she had it her way, tonight was her last trip down to the Chattahoochee River.

As she lathered her body, she couldn't help but wonder why Vincent didn't get her message. Elizabeth didn't look too pleased to see her, and if her instincts were correct, there was a storm brewing on the horizon for the newly dating couple.

***

After putting Cherise's clothes in the washer, Vincent made his way to the bedroom and pulled a crisp, white T-shirt out of his dresser and a pair of his gym shorts. When he walked into the spare bedroom, he noticed Cherise's cell phone sitting on the bed. He picked it up and looked though her outbound call list. As expected, he saw where she had called his house at exactly ten forty-five P.M. His suspicions were correct; not that he didn't believe Cherise anyway. Now all he had to do was get Elizabeth to admit to the obvious and cut his losses before feelings got hurt.

On his way into the living room, he cracked the door to the bathroom and said, "C. J., your clothes are in the washer, and I left you something to put on in the bedroom."

"Thanks," she yelled from the shower.

In the living room, Vincent slowly walked over to Elizabeth, who was sitting on the sofa, watching TV.

She held her glass up to her lips and sarcastically asked, "Did you get Cherise settled in?"

"Yeah, she's all set," he answered as he sat down next to her. "What I want to know is why you erased her voice message."

Startled by his accusation, she turned to him and said, "I don't know what you're talking about. She must've dialed a wrong number."

He calmly said, "Don't lie to me, Elizabeth. I checked Cherise's cell phone. She called nearly an hour ago, and my number's programmed in her phone. There's no way she could dial wrong."

Elizabeth set her glass on the coffee table and said, "I don't like what you're implying, Vincent."

"Good, because I'm not implying anything. You had to have erased her message because there's no one else here who could've done it."

When she opened her mouth to speak, he put his hand up to stop her. "Elizabeth, stop before you dig yourself into a deeper hole." That's when the police officer in him really came out. "I have an extension in my bedroom, and her number shows up on the caller ID. I guess you didn't think about that, huh?"

Elizabeth lowered her head, indicating defeat. She had acted so hastily she didn't think her actions through before carrying them out.

"Why would you erase her message?" he asked softly.

She looked up at him with tears in her eyes and said, "I just wanted some alone time with you, Vincent."

He looked away and said, "I don't get it, Elizabeth. You're here. We're having a good time, and were about to have an even better time."

"That's my point, Vincent. Things were going great until she arrived."

Confused, he asked, "What does my sister-in-law being here have to do with us?"

"Don't act like you don't know what I'm talking about. There's no way you're going to have sex with me with her here."

He laughed and asked, "Why not? I've done it before, and I'm sure you've done it in hotels countless times with people staying in the next room."

"It's not the same thing. She's a part of your family, and it's all about privacy. I wouldn't be comfortable, and it's my first time being here with you."

Vincent rubbed his hands together, a gesture he often did to calm himself when he was angry. "I don't know what to think about you anymore. Cherise is family, and I don't like it when someone mistreats her. What if it had been an emergency?"

"I'm sorry, Vincent. I never looked at it like I was mistreating her. She didn't say she was coming over. She just said to call her back if you were home."

He put his arm around her shoulders and pointed his finger in her face. "It doesn't matter what she said. You erased her message, and that pisses me off."

With tears streaming down her face, she wrapped her arms around his neck and said, "I made one stupid little mistake. Can't you forgive me?"

He removed her arm and said, "I think we need to call it a night. I'm going to have to get you a cab, because we both had too much to drink, so I can't drive you home."

"I was hoping I would get to spend the night with you, Vincent."

He picked up the telephone and said, "Me too, but you ruined that when you intercepted C. J.'s telephone call."

Vincent called downstairs to the guard and asked him to call a cab for Elizabeth.

"I'm sorry the night has to end like this. I'll walk you down and sit with you until the cab arrives."

She grabbed her purse and angrily charged toward the door. "Don't do me any favors. I know my way out."

He stood in the middle of the floor and watched her slam the door. He followed her down the hallway and to the elevator. The ride down to the lobby was quiet, and when the doors opened, a cab was already waiting for her in front of the building. She walked at a faster pace ahead of him and said, "You don't have to walk me to the car."

"Yes, I do. I want to pay the fare."

She turned to him and pointed her finger in his face. "I'm not your charity case. I can pay my own way."

"I know you can, but you were my date tonight, which makes me responsible for you. End of discussion."

Vincent handed the cab driver a fifty dollar bill and said, "Make sure she gets home safe. You can keep the change."

"Thank you, sir," the cab driver replied before tucking the money in his pocket.

Elizabeth reached down to open the car door, but Vincent stopped her.

"You're a beautiful, intelligent woman, Elizabeth, but you need to get your insecurities in check. I'm really disappointed how you handled things tonight."

She swung the car door open and said, "Spare me the sympathy, Vincent. God gave women a sixth sense, and I know something's going on with you and Cherise."

He chuckled and said, "Whatever, but for the record, I don't have to explain or justify my relationship with Cherise to you. Do me a favor and call me when you get home so I'll know you made it safely."

Elizabeth nodded in silence. Vincent leaned in the window and gave her a subtle kiss on the lips.

"Good night, Elizabeth."

"Good night, Vincent," she replied before the cab driver pulled away from the curb.

Upstairs, Cherise sat down on the side of the bed and set her alarm to go off in three hours. Vincent walked past her door on the way to his bedroom.

"Commander, where are you going?"

He stepped inside the room and said, "I'm just putting my keys and wallet up. Are you getting ready to turn in?"

"Yeah," she answered as she rubbed lotion on her arms. "Where's Elizabeth?"

"Gone."

"I'm sorry, Vincent. I only used the key you gave me because I didn't think you were home."

He walked farther into the room and leaned against the dresser. He picked up a small figurine and said, "I gave you that key for a reason. You're free to use my place any time you need to. It's close to your office, and it wouldn't make sense to drive all the way home to get cleaned up or take a nap between shifts."

"I know, but I should've tried to call again before I just let myself in. I was embarrassed, and so was Elizabeth."

Vincent set the figurine down and said, "She'll be all right. We weren't doing anything anyway."

Cherise laughed and said, "It didn't look like it to me. The woman could barely get her blouse back on. She was so embarrassed."

He laughed and said, "I guess it was a Kodak moment, huh?"

"Uh, yeah!" Cherise replied.

"It's all good, so stop apologizing. Shit happens, but the fact remains that she lied about your call and admitted to erasing it."

Surprised, Cherise asked, "Why would she erase it?"

He smiled, showing his handsome dimples. "She claimed she wanted some alone time with me."

Cherise smiled and said, "That's a good reason. I can't say I blame her. I think she's in love with you, Vincent."

"Please!"

She walked across the room and put the lotion back in her purse. His eyes followed her body as the light hit the T-shirt just right, giving him a clear silhouette of her sexy body.

"Think about it. For a woman to go as far as to erase a message so she could be alone with you, she was on a mission. I honestly think she's trying to get you to the altar."

"Well, that ain't happening, and she worked her ass right out the door. That's why she's on her way home in a cab."

Cherise climbed under the comforter and said, "You're mean, Vincent."

"I'm not mean. I'm just keeping it real," he said as he hit the light switch, turning out the light. "Go to bed, woman. I'll put your clothes in the dryer when it stops."

"Thanks," she replied before lying down on the pillow. Within minutes, she was sound asleep.

Chapter Twelve

Two hours into her power nap, Cherise was startled out of her sleep after having a bizarre dream. She sat up on the side of the bed and wiped her eyes. For the past few nights, she'd dreamed that Mason's stalker had come after her with a knife, and it was unbelievably violent and real. She just prayed that it wasn't a premonition. She was always cautious, but the dreams were keeping her more than alert when she was away from home.

Vincent's house was extremely quiet, so she figured he was sound asleep. She didn't want to disturb him, so she made her way into the kitchen for a drink of water before trying to squeeze out another hour and a half of sleep. In the hallway, she stepped into the laundry room and found that Vincent had her clothes already hanging up and ready to go. The house was dark, and the only light was from the recessed lighting over the bar. She opened the refrigerator and found an array of juices and other delicious items, but she was thirsty for water. When she pulled the bottle from the refrigerator, she noticed a container full of pineapple, watermelon, grapes, cantaloupe, and honeydew melon. She only wanted a spoonful, but once she took a bite, she ending up eating a bowlful. When she turned to put her empty container in the sink, she was startled to find Vincent staring at her in the darkness of the hallway.

"Hungry?" he asked softly.

She wiped her mouth and said, "Just a little bit. Your fruit is delicious."

"You know me. I only buy the best."

"I hope you don't mind me taking a bite."

He smiled and said, "I told you what's mine is yours. You know that."

"Did I wake you?"

He slowly moved out of the darkness into soft light and said, "No, I couldn't sleep."

Within seconds, he was staring down at her with his lips in inches of hers. He savored the floral smell of her lotion and her sweet breath. Her lips were magnetic, drawing him even closer to her. Cherise swallowed hard as chills began to run all over her body, especially when he began to caress her cheek ever so gently with his finger. She could feel his warm breath and the heat of his body as he continued to stroke her cheek. His eyes were full of love as he slowly covered her lips with his.

He thought about the conversation he'd had with Mason regarding their affair, and realized he was being a hypocrite, but he couldn't resist the undeniable love he had for her no matter how hard he tried.

Cherise was so stunned by Vincent's actions that she was frozen where she stood. Tears welled up in her eyes, and her heart pounded in her chest. The blood running through her veins felt like it was boiling hot and ice cold at the same time, and when his lips touched her body, she shivered uncontrollably.

"Vincent . . ." she softly called out to him.

He kissed her once more then breathlessly asked, "Do you want me to stop?"

"In my mind, yes, but in my heart, no."

He stared into her confused eyes for a second and then released her. As he took a step back from her, he said, "Go to bed, C. J."

"I'm sorry, Vincent."

"You have nothing to be sorry for," he replied as he turned and began to walk down the hallway to his bedroom.

After watching him close the door, only then did she realize she had been holding her breath. Then, in an instant, her heart took over her mind, and before she knew it, she was opening his bedroom door.

"May I come in?" she asked softly.

The room was dark, but she could still see him moving around under the gold satin sheets.

He rolled over to face her, and with a less than enthusiastic tone, asked, "What do you want?"

She walked toward the bed without responding, and eased under the sheets beside him.

"I see you still like playing with fire," he whispered as he wrapped his arm around her waist, pulling her closer to his body.

"I love you, Vincent," she whispered softly in the darkness as she laid her head on his chest.

"I know you do, but if you don't get out of my bed in the next ten seconds, I won't be responsible for my actions."

Tears rolled out of her eyes as his words sank in. She knew she had overstepped the boundaries she'd set for them, but she'd been there before, and was well aware of the consequences.

"I know what I'm doing," she replied as she nuzzled her face against his warm neck. "I'm not going anywhere."

He rolled on top of her, and before kissing her softly, said, "Your ten seconds is up."

Cherise wrapped her arms around his neck and returned

his loving kisses as he slowly relieved her of her shorts and T-shirt. She trembled when his hands and lips caressed every inch of her soft body. He watched her reaction when he paid special attention to her most feminine areas. His body was solid and throbbing, and he could hardly prolong his loving, but he had to, because he didn't want it to end before it started.

Breathless, Cherise cupped his face and pleaded, "Vincent . . ."

"Not yet," he answered right before he dipped his head and disappeared between her thighs. Cherise whimpered loudly as his lips and tongue explored her feminine core with expert precision. He was an artist, and he knew exactly when to partake of her sweetness and when to pull back.

Her moans and whimpers increased, and her body trembled as he showed no signs of letting up. She begged for mercy as she gripped the bed linens, but he was just getting started. He wanted her to reach the ultimate peak of satisfaction, one that would render her completely out of control and at his mercy. He'd seen it before, and it was absolutely amazing. Until then, she had to succumb to the undeniable pleasure bestowed upon her. It seemed endless, and he was enjoying it just as much as she was.

His action made her say things she hadn't said in a long time, as well as promise things she'd never promised before. Hearing exactly what he already knew allowed him to torture her a few more minutes, until he witnessed her experience a series of long, hard orgasms.

He took great pleasure in seeing his woman satisfied and speechless, so he quickly pulled a condom out of the nightstand and then moved between her legs. He ran his tongue over her brown peaks, devouring them at times.

"I can't stand not being able to love you like I want to."

She was speechless as tears spilled out of her eyes. Mason had caused her so much anxiety, stress, and pain. Lately she felt like she deserved to feel unbridled passion from the one man she had no doubt loved her.

"We have tonight, Vincent. Just make it count."

All the forbidden love between them was released with explosive force as he propelled his muscular frame into her body and soul. They spent the next hour and a half tangled in each other's arms. Elizabeth was right; there was something between him and Cherise, and it was something neither she nor any other woman would ever come close to matching.

He made love to her with such fever that the only thing that could stop him was the building catching fire or death. Cherise would regret her request to make it count, because her body shuddered so hard that she caught severe muscle cramps in both legs. Vincent was winded, but he had a lot of energy left in him. His body glistened with perspiration as he gave his lover a temporary break, only so he could massage the cramps out of her thighs.

"Spend the night with me."

With her voice barely above a whisper, she replied, "I can't. I have to go back to work."

He ran his hands over the curve of her hips, caressing her firm bottom. "I promise I'll let you sleep."

"No, you won't. You're pawing at me now," she joked.

"I can't help myself," he admitted. "Call in sick. I haven't had enough of you yet."

She turned to him and said, "I can't. You do know we're right back where we started, don't you?"

He trailed kisses down to her navel and back up to her lips. "What does that say about how we feel about each other?"

She looked into his eyes and said, "I agree, but I can't just walk up to Mason and tell him I'm in love with you and announce that our marriage is over. I have to think about the children too."

He rolled onto his back and stared at the ceiling. His mind was racing a hundred miles an hour. Cherise was right. Mason had already admitted that he was still a little paranoid about their relationship, and now his paranoia had been proven right.

"At some point, we're going to have to be honest with Mason, and you need to understand that it's not going to be pretty," he revealed to her. "If I thought he wanted to kill me before, he won't hesitate to really do it this time."

"I don't want things to get violent because of me," she replied. "I'd rather be by myself than to have you two drawing blood."

Vincent laughed. "Have you forgotten you're married to a black man? I know my brother. He is not going to take this well at all."

She swallowed the lump in her throat and said, "I can handle Mason. I'm more worried about my children. Mason and I have tried to hold our marriage together for the longest, but the fact that I'm here with you proves that it's failed."

"It's not your fault," he pointed out. Stop the guilt trip. We've all had a role in this thing, but right now, I have to know if you're serious about us. If you want to stay with Mason and continue to work on your marriage, then I'm out. I can't live like this anymore. If you're in love with me like you say you are and want to be together, we'll have to figure out how to break the news to Mason and the children."

Cherise sat up and put his T-shirt over her head in silence. She walked over to the window and stared out at the downtown lights. He joined her at the window and hugged her from behind. The moment his body came in contact with hers, she felt an electrifying sensation. A sensation only he had been able to give her.

She turned to him and said, "Mason has to hear the truth from me."

"No. I don't want you to do it alone."

"He won't hurt me," she replied as she took his hand into hers and kissed it. "I'm the only one who can break the news to him. I owe him that much."

"He'll kill you, C. J."

"No, he won't," she answered. "He'll be pissed, but I know Mason better than you think I do. He knows he's not without guilt, and that he had a huge part in destroying our marriage. Don't worry. I can handle it."

Vincent stepped away from her and studied her calmness. She might believe she knew her husband, but men don't take their wives' infidelity well, even if they have been unfaithful themselves; and since a family member was involved, that made it worse. There would be hell to pay, but from whom and by whom would remain a mystery for now.

She moved away from him and said, "I have to go to work."

"Are you sure you can't stay?" he asked as he followed her.

She turned on the shower and said, "I wish I could, but I can't."

He pulled the T-shirt over her head, exposing her curvy body to him. As his eyes scanned her lovely figure, he couldn't resist pulling her into his arms for a fiery kiss. She broke the kiss and stepped into the shower, pulling him inside with her.

"Can you do my back for me?"

He closed the sliding door to the huge shower and smothered her with kisses. "I plan to do a lot more than your back."

She did eventually return to work that night, but an hour

later than she had planned, only because she didn't want to leave Vincent's arms. It was a trying night for both of them, and one she would never forget.

Later that afternoon, Cherise found Mason in the bedroom, packing a suitcase. She set her purse on the chair and asked, "Where are you headed?"

"I have to go to New York tonight to check out a lead on a case," he answered without making eye contact with her. What he didn't want her to know was that he was flying into New York and then driving to D.C. to meet Lillian so he could have a DNA test done on her daughter.

"New York? How long will you be gone?" she asked curiously.

"I don't know, sweetheart. Hopefully, it's just going to be a day or two. I'll know more once I get there and brief the other detectives. That's why I'm packing extra clothes, just in case."

"I see," she replied as she made her way into their closet. "When did you find out you had to go?"

Mason walked into the closet and pulled a belt off a hanger. "I found out this afternoon. I called your office and your cell and left you messages to call. This case we're working on started moving quickly after we got some new information."

She watched him move around their bedroom, double-checking his suitcase for necessities. "I got your messages, but I was already on my way home. I hope you're able to close the case."

He glance up at her and said, "Me too. By the way, I heard those Chattahoochee River shootings are keeping you busy. How's the investigation going?"

"Not as fast as I'd like it to. We have some bullet casings, tire tracks, and footprints. There's a lot of trash on the banks of the river, so it's hard to tell which items are part of the crime scene and what's not. All I know is that I'm tired and glad I'm off tomorrow—and not on call."

He kissed her forehead and said, "You've been working too hard. I'll order the kids a pizza before I leave so you won't have to worry about cooking."

"Thank you, Mason," she replied as she hugged his waist. "Listen, when you get back, I need to talk to you about a few things."

He looked at his watch and said, "I have a little time now if you want to talk."

A lump appeared in her throat as she nervously caressed his hands.

"No, it can wait until you get back. I want you to stay focused on your case. Just call when you land so I'll know you made it safely."

He cupped her face and stared into her sad, weary eyes. "You look exhausted."

"I am. It's been a tough few days," she admitted without revealing that her exhaustion was the combination of her long work schedule and a passion-filled night with Vincent.

"Why don't you run yourself a hot bath and relax," he suggested as he slowly unbuttoned her shirt for her and pushed it off her shoulders. "The kids are not babies anymore, so you don't have to supervise them like in the past. They know their responsibilities."

"I think I'm going to take you up on that."

"Get some rest," he said softly before giving her a loving kiss on the lips.

It was going to be harder than ever for her to break his heart. He was so loving and gentle when he wasn't being deceptive, mysterious, and distant.

"I will."

He zipped up his suitcase and said, "Double check the house before you turn in for the night."

She nodded and then asked, "Do you want me to walk you out?"

"No, sweetheart, go take your bath. I'll get Mase to lock up and set the alarm."

"Good luck on the case."

"Thanks. I'm going to need it," he answered as he winked at her. "I love you."

"I love you too," she replied with sincerity before retiring into the bathroom.

Chapter Thirteen

Mason stepped off the plane in LaGuardia Airport after the two and a half hour flight and yawned. It was nearly eight o'clock, and he still had a long drive ahead of him. He wanted to get this visit over as soon as possible, so he could get back to Atlanta and his family.

As he made his way to the rental car pavilion, he yawned again. He hadn't realized how tired he was. That's when he decided to get a hotel room and start fresh in the morning. Lillian was unaware that he was coming, and he thought it was best not to call ahead. He wasn't looking forward to the two hundred mile drive to D.C., but it was necessary that he flew into New York instead of D.C. in order to cover his tracks. He also made sure that he had plenty of cash on him to use while he was in D.C. so he wouldn't have to use his credit cards.

Once he got his car, he drove directly to the nearby Crowne Plaza Hotel and checked in. It was a typical chilly night in New York, and after yawning a few more times, he finally got his key, climbed into the elevator, and slowly made his way to his room for a good night's sleep. Before turning in for the night, he called Cherise to say good night.

The next morning, Mason hit I-95 and made his way south

toward D.C. He made the trip in record time because he was anxious to have the paternity tests. He had researched testing facilities and found a respectable lab that could do the testing in a timely fashion.

When he got close to Lillian's neighborhood, only then did he call her and let her know he was five minutes from her house. He had looked up her address on the police database before leaving Atlanta. She sounded a little nervous over the telephone, but her nervousness wasn't showing when she opened the door and greeted him by throwing herself in his arms.

"I'm not here for that, Lillian," Mason said as he removed her arms. "Why don't you put on some clothes?"

She was dressed in some very revealing shorts and a sports bra.

"You've seen me in less than this. Besides, I'm home. Damn! You used to love seeing me in next to nothing."

He stepped into her family room and said, "I'm here on business . . . period."

She hugged his waist and said, "You say that now, but I know you, baby."

Mason laughed and stepped out of her embrace and sat down. "You used to know me."

Lillian sat down and asked, "So, how long are you going to be in town?"

"Only long enough to get the DNA test done and I'm out."

She massaged his shoulders and said, "Well, I'm glad you're here, and I hope you stay awhile."

Mason looked around the room and asked, "So, where's your daughter?"

"*Our* daughter is in Kentucky with my mother. She won't be back until the end of the week."

He sighed and said, "Kentucky? Why isn't she in school?"

"If you must know, I'm having her home schooled since she's been so sick. Her teacher comes three times a week."

"I came all the way up here for nothing," he replied with somewhat of an attitude.

"It's not my fault you didn't call to let me know you were coming. Baby, I love you, but you can't just show up at my doorstep any time you feel like it. I have guidelines too."

Mason stood and said, "That's cool, and I'm sorry I didn't call ahead, but you've been acting kind of weird lately, so I was being cautious."

"You have no reason to fear me, baby," she replied with her arms around his waist.

"Well, there's no sense in me hanging around here now. I'll try to come back in a week or two."

Lillian held on to him tighter. She didn't want to let him go. She finally had him in her territory, and if things went her way, it would be forever. She just had to play her cards right.

"I would love it if you stayed a few days. I could call my mom and see if I could fly her back sooner."

Frustrated, he pushed her away and said, "I'm not going to hang around D.C. for a week. If you can get her back in a couple of days, great. If not, I'll have to come back another time."

"I could give you a strand of her hair, but I know that won't be enough for you. I know you want to see her for yourself, and I can't blame you. She's beautiful, Mason, and she's the product of our love."

Mason studied Lillian's behavior. While she was an extremely sexy woman, maybe he'd made a mistake by showing up unannounced. The last thing he wanted to do was give her false hope of a relationship. Their sordid past was hot, sleazy, and uninhibited, and whether he wanted to believe it or not, he did have some deep-seated feelings for her.

"I have to go, Lillian. It's been a long trip and I'm tired."

She caressed his neck and said, "I know you're tired, but while you're here, we could grab some lunch and hang out."

Mason's stomach growled as soon as she mentioned food, but he was a little apprehensive about being alone with Lillian. He was hungry, since he'd only had a bagel and a cup of coffee before hitting the road that morning, so a nourishing meal would do him some good before relaxing for the rest of the day.

"Lunch actually sounds good," he answered. "What do you have a taste for?"

She looked into his eyes mischievously before glancing down at his crotch. "You know not to ask me that question, but whatever you want to eat is okay with me," she replied in a seductive manner.

He laughed and said, "I thought you said you were going to behave."

She walked into her kitchen and grabbed a stack of carry-out menus and said, "I am behaving, sweetheart. Would you like to see McKenzie's room before we eat?"

He set the menus on the table and said, "Sure."

Mason followed Lillian upstairs and down the hallway to a room decorated with a jungle theme, inclusive of a mural of trees and a straw hut on the wall.

"This is nice," Mason said as he walked farther into the room. "She must love animals."

Lillian sat on her daughter's bed and picked up a large stuffed elephant. "Mason, she's so special and so beautiful. She's just like you. The zoo is her favorite place."

He walked over to a small desk, where he picked up a picture of Lillian and her daughter. "This is a nice picture."

"It would've been nicer if you could've been in the picture."

"That's impossible and you know that."

"Nothing's impossible where we're concerned," Lillian answered.

He set the picture back down and said, "She's beautiful, Lillian."

Lillian smiled with admiration. McKenzie was everything to her, and so was Mason. All she had to do was get him to see the truth, and they could be a family once and for all.

Mason walked toward the door and said, "If we're going to get something to eat, we'd better pick something out."

Lillian and Mason went through the menus, and after a short discussion, they decided to go out to lunch instead. Lillian quickly changed into a denim skirt and sexy, low cut blouse before heading out the door with Mason.

A few hours later, Lillian accompanied Mason to a downtown hotel, where he checked in to his room for the evening.

"This is nice," she observed as she stretched out across his bed. "This bed is so soft and big. I could stay in it with you for hours."

He chuckled and said, "You're not staying in my room, so don't start trippin'."

She giggled and said, "I don't know why you're so sensitive. Most men love it when a woman flirts with them."

"There's nothing harmless about your flirting. You play dirty, Lillian."

She walked over to him, swaying her hips along the way. "Stop being such a party pooper. I don't know why you're staying in this hotel anyway. You're more than welcome to stay at my house."

He opened his suitcase and took out his toiletries and took them into the bathroom.

"Thanks, but no thanks."

"You have a nice view of the city," she noted as she pulled back the curtains.

He joined her at the window and said, "I love D.C. It has the old and new mixed together. The city has a nice vibe, especially with Obama in the White House."

She turned to him, and out of nowhere, seriously asked, "What are you going to do once the DNA proves McKenzie's your daughter? Are you going to help me get her a kidney?"

"I can't think that far ahead. Right now, I'm only here to have the DNA test done."

"This is a waste of time. Do you really think I would lie to you about having your child?"

He looked her in the eyes and said, "No, but I have to be sure for my sake. It's going to devastate my wife. She doesn't deserve any more heartache."

Lillian frowned and said, "Thanks for ruining the mood. Don't you care about me at all?"

He turned to Lillian and said, "I'm not going to have this conversation with you. You've always known I was married, so stop being a drama queen."

She didn't like hearing him talk about his wife with so much conviction. It angered her a little bit; his wife wasn't here, and she was, so she was going to do everything in her power to change his mind and make him realize she was the better woman for him. She quickly changed gears.

"I'm just glad you're here, Mason," she said with a smile.

Surprisingly, it felt good to hold Lillian again. She'd been acting so erratically lately, he didn't know what to expect from her once he arrived today, but so far, so good. This was the

Lillian he remembered and had feelings for. She was beautiful, full of confidence, and extremely sexy, and before he realized it, he felt his heart flutter. If he was the father of Lillian's daughter, it was going to be a tough conversation to have with Cherise, and he realized it could possibly ruin his marriage once and for all.

"Are you ready to go?" Mason asked her after pulling his car keys out of his pocket.

"Whenever you are," she replied with a smile. "Thanks again for taking me to lunch."

He opened the door to his hotel room and said, "It was my pleasure."

They made their way out of the hotel, but before returning to Lillian's house, she talked him into a short tour around the city. When he finally pulled into her driveway, he put the car in park and said, "Call me tomorrow and let me know if your mom can get your daughter here before I have to fly back to Atlanta."

"Where are you headed after you leave here?"

"I'm going back to the hotel and chill. It's been a long day."

She took his hand and asked, "Why don't you come in and rest here? We could watch a movie, have a beer, and catch up on things."

He rubbed his chin and said, "I don't think that's a good idea for obvious reasons."

"Please?" she begged. "It would mean a lot to me. I miss talking to you, Mason. When I came to Atlanta, I wasn't there to cause you any problems. I'll admit that I went about things the wrong way, but I am jealous of your wife. She gets to sleep beside you every night. I love you, Mason. I always have and I always will, and I can't forget you as easy as you've been able to forget about me."

He looked at her and saw the tears in her eyes. "I haven't forgotten you, Lillian. We had a good time, and you're cool with me, as long as you stop with the crazy stuff."

Lillian wiped her eyes and nodded in agreement.

He looked into her beautiful eyes and saw a soft side to Lillian. He considered everything she said, because at one time, he was basically living with her. But he was still upset about her cutting Cherise's tires and showing up at his house. For a man, that was always a no-no.

"All right, Lillian, if you be cool, I'll stay cool. No more showing up at my house or going near my wife or children. I'm going to try to help you get through this situation with your daughter and—"

"Our daughter," she replied, cutting him off.

He sighed and said, "Like I said before, I need undeniable proof."

"That's fair," she answered. "So, are you going to hang out with me or not?"

He pointed at her and said, "Only for a little while."

Lillian clapped her hands together and hugged his neck with excitement, but he vowed to himself that if things got out of hand, he was out of there with a quickness.

It was nearly seven o'clock before Mason realized it. He and Lillian had watched a high energy action movie and ordered Chinese for dinner. Her refrigerator was stocked with plenty of food, beer, and wine, so after a couple of bottles of beer, Mason's long day finally caught up with him.

"Are you okay?" she asked as she massaged his neck.

"I'm good," he replied as he looked at his watch. "I need to get going. I didn't mean to stay over here this long."

"I enjoyed your company today," she said as she linked her arm with his. "It feels good to have you back."

He rubbed his weary eyes and said, "I'm not back, Lillian."

Then, without the slightest hesitation, she took his hand into hers, kissed it, and guided his hand under her skirt. When his hand came in contact with her body, he realized she wasn't wearing any panties.

"Do you remember this, baby?" she asked him seductively as she stared into his eyes.

Mason lowered his head and then removed his hand. "You promised you were going to behave."

She smiled and said, "I am behaving. Mason, I know I can make you happy. I miss you so much. My heart and my body ache for you every second of every day. Make love to me."

"I can't. Those days are behind me. I'm going to be faithful to my wife."

She took his hand and placed it between her legs once again so he could feel the heat radiating from her body. "That sounds sweet and all, but who's going to know? Nobody's here but me and you," she said as she ran her tongue across his lips, a trick she'd done many times before. She knew it would instantly arouse him.

Weakening, he closed his eyes and prayed for strength to get him out of the situation.

He had to admit that her body felt wonderful, and she was doing every trick she had to break him down. Surprisingly, it was working.

"It's just you and me, Mason," she whispered over and over as she held his hand against her heat. "Let yourself go, baby, and just enjoy the moment. Enjoy me. I'm yours and you're mine. Can't you feel it?"

He shook his head to try to regain his composure, but he

was at his breaking point, and mechanically began to slowly caress her center. Lillian let out a soft sigh and continued to coach him through their foreplay. Mason could hear his heart beating loudly in his chest, and his skin felt like it was on fire.

"I can't do this," he whispered softly to her, but his pleas were falling on deaf ears.

"You're already doing it, baby, and it feels so good," she replied breathlessly as her moans heightened in intensity.

He inserted his finger, and then all of his sensibility and resistance went out the window.

Lillian moaned even louder and Mason's eyes glazed over as he continued to fondle her. His lower region was now visible through his slacks, and Lillian began to gyrate her hips against his large hand.

He was pleasing her just with the touch of his hand, but Lillian wanted more. She lay back on the sofa and pulled her blouse over her head and removed her bra, exposing her size-D breasts to her lover.

Mason immediately palmed her breasts with his other hand and began to pinch her nipples. His eyes were bloodshot and full of water as his shaft strained against his zipper. He stared down at her breasts and then quickly covered them with his warm lips.

Lillian let out a loud sigh as he greedily moved from one breast to the other, giving them equal attention. She smiled with satisfaction because she had her man exactly where she wanted him, and she knew there was no turning back as she held him in her arms.

Mason's resistance had gone up in smoke. He quickly yanked her skirt up over her hips, dipped his head between her large thighs, and then let his tongue do the talking for him. Lillian dangled her legs over his shoulders, giving him full access to her heated center as she held his head in place. Her eyes rolled back in her head and she moaned even louder as he savored her sweet nectar. She never wanted him to stop, but seconds later, she screamed as her body was hit with an amazing orgasm.

Once she had regained her senses, she kissed Mason hard on the lips before sliding down to her knees in front of him. Just before unzipping his pants, she looked up at him and with strong conviction, said, "I love you, Mason McKenzie."

With his chest heaving in anticipation, he touched her cheek lovingly before he laid his head back on the sofa and closed his eyes. Lillian lowered her head in his lap and slowly took in all of him. She increased her motion. The louder he groaned, the longer her tongue danced around the tip of his manhood, before engulfing him over and over and over.

"Lillian," he called out to her as he grabbed fistfuls of her hair. He felt her masterful skills pleasuring him, and nearly lost it when she placed him between her breasts.

She stood and pushed her skirt down to her ankles, leaving her body completely naked. Mason's eyes scanned the length of her shapely figure before pulling her onto his lap. He buried his face between her breasts and said, "You're a goddamn voodoo priestess."

She giggled and kissed him hard on the lips before sticking her tongue in his ear.

"Get a condom," he urgently commanded her with a strained voice.

Lillian reached inside her purse and quickly pulled out a foil packet. She ripped open the packet and put the condom on Mason before pulling him down to the floor on top of her.

Mason quickly moved his hips between her thighs and placed one of her legs over his shoulders. He felt as if her body as magnetic to him, pulling him in, deeper and deeper, making him unable to break free even if he wanted to. He began to vigorously grind his hips into her body, causing her to moan with each thrust.

This was the man she fell in love with finally loving her back, and it felt wonderful as he nibbled on her breasts between precise plunges. Lillian whined and hissed throughout their lovemaking session, exciting Mason to a massive peak. Tears fell out of her eyes when her body spasmed underneath him. Seconds later, he met his own violent release, causing him to let out a loud groan, collapsing on top of her.

Mason never made it back to his hotel room that night. In fact, he ended up making love to Lillian a couple of more times. She had become irresistible once again, despite the fact that he promised Cherise that he would never, ever cheat on her again. Maybe Lillian was a voodoo priestess after all. In any case, she had caused Mason to fall off the wagon and become a sex addict for her all over again.

The next morning, just as the sun peeked over the horizon, Mason slowly awakened to Lillian's oral wake-up call.

"Lillian, you're killing me," he whined as he closed his eyes and enjoyed the immense pleasure she was giving him.

She looked up at him momentarily and softly said, "I'll never get enough of you, or stop loving you. Relax and let me do my thang."

A couple of minutes later, with his body ripe and throbbing, Mason's hands trembled as he opened another foil packet. He positioned himself behind her curvaceous bottom and made love to her once more, bringing Lillian to tears, as well as a fulfilling and orgasmic scream.

Chapter Fourteen

Mason had been out of town for two days, leaving Cherise filled with sadness and anxiety over telling him about her affair. Vincent had serious feelings of concern for Cherise's safety if she revealed their affair to his brother alone, and would prevent her from doing so at all costs. Since their passionate night together, the two hadn't hooked up. Not because they didn't want to, but because they needed time to think about the future and how their news was going to be received by Mason and the children.

Vincent had made up his mind that he was going to be the one to tell Mason about the affair instead of Cherise. He'd left countless messages on Mason's cell phone, but Mason had yet to return any of the calls. Unbeknownst to Vincent, Mason was still in D.C. with Lillian. Vincent decided to call Cherise to find out where he was.

"C. J. McKenzie."

"C. J., is Mason still in New York? I've been trying to reach him for two days."

Cherise hesitated then said, "Well, hello to you too."

He chuckled and said, "I'm sorry. Hello, beautiful. How are you?"

"That's much better, and I'm fine, thank you," she answered. "And yes, he's still in New York."

"I see. Have you talked to him?"

Before she could answer him, she was interrupted briefly by a member of her CSI team. After answering her team member's question, she turned her attention back to Vincent.

"I'm sorry, Vincent. I'm working a scene," she revealed. "I haven't talked to Mason today, but he called last night."

"When is he coming home?" Vincent asked.

"He didn't say, and I didn't ask. I stopped asking a long time ago."

He sighed and said, "I don't want you telling him about us until I've had a chance to talk to him."

"This is my responsibility," she reminded him. "It won't be right if he doesn't hear it from me."

"Forget it, C.J. Listen, if Mason calls you, tell him I'm trying to get in touch with him."

"Seriously, Vincent, stay out of it."

"I'm all up in it, babe. I got this."

Cherise was getting a headache, but she didn't have time to argue with him. "Vincent, I can't talk about this right now. I'll call you later, but do me a favor and don't say anything to Mason about us."

"Sweetheart, when I talk to my brother, it will be face to face, so stop stressing. Call me when you finish your scene. I want to see you."

"I want to see you too, but Mase has a basketball game, and I want to take them out to dinner afterwards."

"I almost forgot. Thanks for reminding me," he responded. "I'll see you at the game."

She agreed and hung up the telephone. Vincent decided to do some detective work of his own. He placed a call to Mason's lieutenant and found out that Mason had taken several days off for personal reasons, which deepened the mystery of his whereabouts.

Vincent grabbed his jacket and keys and headed out the door. As he made his way out of the building to his car, his cell phone rang.

"Hello?"

"Hey, bro, I saw where you called. What's up?" Mason casually asked.

"Where the hell are you? Because I know you're not in New York, and I know you're not working on a case," Vincent asked angrily.

"Why are you acting so hostile?" Mason asked. "I just took a few mental health days, that's all."

"If that's true, then why did you have to lie to your wife?" Vincent replied to counter Mason's question.

Mason knew he was busted, so he decided to let Vincent in on his secret trip.

"Okay, stop with the interrogation. I'm in D.C. trying to get a DNA test done with Lillian's daughter," he admitted.

Vincent stopped in his tracks and asked, "Have you lost your damn mind? Why didn't you tell me you were going up there? You know that woman's crazy."

"Hold up, Vincent. Lillian didn't know I was coming either. Everything's cool."

"What do you mean, 'everything's cool'?" Vincent asked. "A few days ago, you was freaking out about her."

"Calm down, bro. I told you I needed to get the DNA tests done. Her daughter's out of town and I'm trying to hang around until she gets back. As soon as we do the test, I'm out."

Vincent climbed into his car and said, "I still don't think that was a smart move."

"I had planned to be back before you even noticed I was gone."

"You still should've told me. If Lillian cut C. J.'s tires and showed up at your house, who knows what else she'll do. I hope you know what you're doing."

Mason chuckled and said, "Don't worry. I have her under control. She won't give me any more trouble."

"How do you know?" Vincent asked.

"Trust me. I know," Mason answered with confidence.

At that moment, Lillian walked into the room and said, "Hey, baby! You ready to go?"

Mason motioned for Lillian to be quiet.

Vincent shook his head and asked, "Is that her?"

"Yeah, that's her."

"What's really going on, Mason?" Vincent asked.

"Nothing," he lied as Lillian climbed into his lap and started kissing his neck. He stood, pushing her out of his lap, and said, "I'm just here for the tests."

Vincent couldn't believe his ears. While he believed Mason was honestly trying to get the DNA tests done, he didn't expect him to actually be with Lillian after all she'd done to him while she was in Atlanta.

"Once again, I hope you know what you're doing."

Mason chuckled and said, "I told you, she's cool. I'll be home soon."

"Good luck," Vincent replied with a hint of concern in his tone.

"Thanks," Mason replied before hanging up. He closed his cell phone and angrily yelled, "You'd better be glad that was Vincent and not my wife I was talking to."

She frowned and said, "My wife! My wife! This is my goddamn house! You don't tell me what to do or say in my own house. You should've told me you were on the goddamn phone."

Mason picked up his keys and said, "You've lost your damn mind."

"No! You lost your damn mind! I'm sick of you throwing your wife in my face every time you get a chance. I know the bitch exists!"

Mason was stunned, but he shouldn't have been. He knew she had a temper, and he knew she had issues with his marriage, but it had been a while since he'd seen her rage and anger.

"I knew I shouldn't have come up here," he stated as he hurried toward the door. "I'm out of here."

In an instant, Lillian's personality changed and she ran over and blocked the door. She had gone from calm and loving to psychotic and furious in less than a minute.

"I'm sorry, baby. I didn't mean it. Don't leave."

Mason tried to push her to the side and open the door, but Lillian threw her arms around his neck and burst into tears. "Don't go! Please! I love you so much. I promise I'll make sure McKenzie's home by tomorrow. Just stay . . . please. I didn't mean what I said."

Mason shoved Lillian to the floor and yelled, "You meant every word of it. This is some bullshit! I'm not staying here any longer. I'll see you in court!"

"Screw you, Mason!" she yelled as she watched him walk out the door, slamming it behind him. She continued to scream out at him even after he had already pulled out of her driveway. "You're going to regret this!" she screamed out one last time before sobbing uncontrollably.

It was nearly an hour later before she pulled herself off the floor and wiped away her tears.

"Oh my God!" she screamed as she circled her sofa. "What have I done? I've lost him! No, I haven't lost him. Mason is my man, and if that's how he wants to play, it's on."

***

Vincent made his way into the high school gym as the two teams warmed up on the floor. Mase spotted his uncle and threw up his hand to greet him as he walked along the court-side toward the home team side of the gym. Vincent stopped to chat briefly with Mase's coach, who was a friend and former college teammate. The two of them had set many records at their alma mater, and Mase and Janelle had inherited all of the McKenzies' athletic abilities.

"Uncle Vincent!" Janelle greeted him excitedly as he made his way up the bleachers. She hugged his neck and gave him a soft kiss on the cheek as he sat down next to Cherise.

"I'm glad you could make it," Cherise said as she smiled over at him.

Vincent winked at her and said, "You know I wouldn't miss my nephew's game if I could help it."

She laughed and said, "Well, he certainly perked up when he saw you."

Vincent looked away and tried to concentrate on the game. He was fighting a strong urge to kiss her. Just sitting next to her was driving him crazy. It didn't help his thought process that his brother was in D.C. with his ex-lover, doing God knows what.

"Momma, when is Daddy coming home?" Janelle asked her mother.

She shifted in her seat, as she had a flashback of the years Mason worked undercover. She couldn't count the number of times her children had asked her that question. To hear it again made her very uncomfortable.

"I don't know, baby," she replied. "If you like, I could send him a text message to find out."

Just then, Janelle saw another child with a delicious-looking hot dog and was instantly distracted from her question. "Momma, may I have a hot dog?" Janelle asked as she rubbed her stomach in anticipation.

"Janelle, we're going out for pizza after the game. Can't you wait?" she asked.

"She's hungry now, and you know what kind of appetite she has," Vincent reminded her as he pulled some cash out of his pocket. "Snacks are on me. What do you say?"

"Please, Momma?" Janelle pleaded as she held her hands together in prayer.

Cherise eventually nodded in agreement and watched as Vincent took Janelle by the hand and they made their way down the bleachers and toward the concession stand.

Cherise watched as Vincent drew the attention of scores of women throughout the gym while he walked down the court with Janelle. She saw some of them staring without discretion, while others whispered and gave each other high five. Vincent was model handsome, and his well-toned physique left little to the imagination as he sported his designer jeans and white button-down shirt. Janelle proudly held his hand as she walked alongside her uncle.

When they returned, Janelle and Vincent not only had hot dogs and soda, but they brought some for Cherise as well.

"Thank you," she said with a smile.

Before taking a bite of his own hot dog, Vincent said, "I knew you were hungry."

She reached over and gave his hand a loving squeeze just as the referee blew his whistle, signaling the tip-off.

The game was a nail-biter, but Mase and his team came out on top, with their star senior hitting a three-point shot at the buzzer. The gym erupted in chaos as students charged out onto the basketball court in celebration. It was a joyous occasion for the team, because it assured them a spot in the upcoming state tournaments. Mase was overjoyed at being a part of the team that was now known as the Sleeping Giants. While their team usually had a winning season, it was this season that they had exceptionally tall players and skills that seemed to come out of nowhere, surprising most area teams, coaches, and sports writers.

After the crowd dissipated a little bit, Vincent, Janelle, and Cherise made their way down to the court to congratulate Mase.

"Good game, nephew," Vincent said as he gave Mase a hug.

"Thanks, Unc!"

Cherise put her arm around her son's shoulders and said, "You did good, son. Congratulations."

"Thank you, Momma."

At that time, a shapely cheerleader ran over to Mase and jumped up in his arms, wrapping her legs around his waist. Cherise's eyes widened in disbelief. She was about to protest when Vincent grabbed her by the arm and pulled her over to the side.

"Chill, C. J. They're just being teenagers."

Cherise frowned and pointed in her son's direction. The cheerleader continued to hug and kiss on Mase, and the celebration got even louder when the band started playing their school song.

"Did you know about this?" Cherise asked Vincent.

He laughed. "Know about what?"

"That girl is all over him! Look at them!" Cherise said with shock.

"They're just celebrating."

"It's obvious you don't see what I see."

Vincent folded his arms and asked, "And what exactly do you see that you didn't see in yourself at that age?"

She punched him in the arm playfully and said, "You're no help."

"Of course not," he replied. "I remember what it felt like to be a teenage boy on a winning team, with all the girls wanting to be with you. It's totally natural, C. J."

They walked toward the door, along with other fans that were starting to file out of the gym.

"I guess you're right. It just seems like Mase is growing up so fast, and these girls are built like women, with their big boobs and round bottoms. It's scary," Cherise admitted.

Vincent pointed over at Janelle and said, "Don't forget you have a daughter that's not too far from being a teenager herself. All you can do is raise them right, talk to them, and pray they make the right decisions."

"I hope you're right." Cherise yawned as she waved Janelle over so they could leave.

"Tired?" he asked.

"Just a little," she answered as she yawned again.

"Why don't you take Janelle home?" he suggested. "I can take Mase out with his teammates."

"That's sweet, Vincent, but you don't have to do that. It's been a long day for you too," she replied as she continued to yawn.

"I know, but I want to. Besides, it'll give me a chance to talk to my homeboy, Coach Windrow."

"Are you sure?" she asked curiously.

He leaned down and gave Janelle a kiss. "Of course I'm sure. I'll bring him home in an hour or so."

"Thank you, Vincent. Let me go tell him good-bye before I leave."

"Can I go with Mase and Uncle Vincent?" Janelle asked her mother as she held tightly to her uncle's hand.

"Janelle, your brother is going out with his teammates. Why don't you let him enjoy the evening with his friends?"

"I'm sure Mase won't mind," Vincent replied. "We can always sit at another table if he wants to chill with his friends."

Cherise pointed at Janelle and said, "If it's okay with your brother, I don't mind."

Happy, Janelle pulled her mother by the hand over to her brother to get his permission, and as expected, he was fine with her tagging along.

When Cherise returned to where Vincent was standing, she found him talking to the single mother of one of the basketball players. The woman was obviously flirting, and couldn't seem to talk to Vincent without patting his hand or arm.

"Excuse me, Vincent. I'm getting ready to go," Cherise announced.

Vincent introduced Cherise to the woman, and together they told her good-bye before walking toward the hallway.

"Mase said he will be out as soon as he finishes his shower."

With his arm around Janelle's shoulders, he said, "Cool. That will give us time to walk you to your truck."

By the time Vincent dropped off the kids, it was nearly midnight, and Cherise was sound asleep on the sofa. Mase opened the door and deactivated the alarm, making a point to be quiet. Janelle ran over to her mother's side and gave her a tender kiss on the cheek, waking her.

"Momma, wake up. We're home," she whispered.

Cherise hugged Janelle's neck and slowly sat up on the sofa. "Hey, baby. What time is it?"

Vincent smiled and walked farther into the room. "It's nearly midnight. Why didn't you go on to bed?"

She pushed the blanket off her body and said, "I wanted to wait up for the kids. Where's Mase?"

"I'm right here," he answered as he stepped into the room holding a bottle of apple juice.

"I think you guys have had enough to eat and drink for the night. It's late, and both of you need to get to bed," she announced as she stood and folded the blanket. "Thank your uncle for putting up with you guys tonight."

Mase gave Vincent a hug and jogged up the stairs. Janelle gave Cherise a quick kiss on the cheek and followed her brother's trail upstairs.

Once the children were gone, Vincent's eyes immediately went to Cherise's shapely body. She was dressed in a set of pajama shorts with a matching tank top, and his eyes were causing her body to react to him.

"Have you talked to Mason?" Vincent asked curiously.

She sighed and said, "Only for a second. He didn't sound good, and I couldn't get him to tell me what was wrong."

Cherise's revelation concerned Vincent. "What do you mean, he didn't sound good?"

"You know . . . he sounded stressed, worried, emotional," she revealed. "Do you think he knows about us?"

"No, I don't, so get that out of your head," Vincent said to comfort her. "Did he say when he would be home?"

"I only talked to him for a minute," she answered as she straightened the pillows on the sofa. "He rushed me off the telephone and told me he loved me."

Vincent touched her cheek lovingly and said, "I'm sure he's fine and will be back soon."

She folded her arms across her chest and said, "I hope you're right."

"I know I'm right, and I'm still serious about you not telling him about us alone."

Cherise linked her arm with his and guided him toward the front door. She didn't want to get into a conversation with him on that level in her house, with the children right upstairs.

She opened the door and said, "Thanks again for taking the kids to dinner. I didn't realize how tired I was until I got home."

He couldn't take his eyes off her lips, and was distracted by her beauty and the floral scent of her lotion. "It was my pleasure."

"Go home and get some rest."

"I'm tired, but never too tired for you."

Cherise opened the front door and looked over her shoulder to make sure the children weren't nearby. "Not now, Vincent."

"I know," he answered before giving her a tender kiss on the corner of the lips. "Sweet dreams."

Chapter Fifteen

Mason's drive back to New York was long, depressing, and lonely. He didn't want to stay another minute in D.C., so he packed his bag and hit the road. As he sat in his hotel room, he tried his best to erase the memories of the past few days, but he couldn't. Lillian's erratic behavior had once again taken him by surprise. Now he had no idea what she would do next. It amazed him how she could be so sweet and loving one minute, and crazed and hostile the next.

As he sat on the side of the bed, he realized she had all the classic signs of bipolar disorder. Lillian had always had mood swings, but they'd gotten worse, and so unpredictable.

Mason looked over at his cell phone and thought about calling Cherise back. He'd rushed her off the cell phone earlier because he was still reeling from his altercation with Lillian. Now he craved to hear her loving voice. In fact, he needed to hear it, but he was sure she was asleep. After contemplating calling her for a few seconds, he gave in and dialed her cell.

"Mason?" she answered in a sleepy voice.

"Hey, sweetheart. I'm sorry I woke you," he apologized.

"It's okay. Where are you?" she asked curiously.

"I'm still in New York."

His answers were short and somewhat troubling in nature, but she didn't want to worry unnecessarily.

Cherise turned over to look at her clock and saw that it was nearly three A.M.

"How's the case going?" she asked trying to generate con-versation.

Mason's hands began to tremble as his nerves started to get the best of him once again.

"It's been tough, but I'm making some progress. If all goes well, I'll be home tomorrow."

Cherise sat up in bed and turned on the lamp. There was a few seconds of silence between them, until Mason asked about the children.

"The kids are fine. Janelle asked about you when we were at Mase's game tonight."

"Did they win?"

"They did, and your son scored twelve points."

Mason let out a breath and said, "I hate that I missed it. Let them know I called."

"I will," she answered. "You sound exhausted. Are you sure you're okay?"

He struggled with his answers, which was so unlike him. He'd worked undercover with drug dealers for years, and had been in worse situations than the one with Lillian; but there was something about her demeanor that had shaken him to the core.

"Yeah, baby, I'm sure. I love you."

"I love you too."

"I'm sorry I disturbed you."

"It's okay, Mason. You didn't disturb me. I'm glad you called. Try to get some sleep, okay?"

He rubbed his weary eyes and stood. "I will. Good night, babe."

"Good night, Mason."

Mason hung up his cell and thought about his situation. He realized he needed to take the control out of Lillian's hands and put the matter to rest once and for all. He had to tell Cherise everything. Once it was out in the open, they could go on with their lives. Whether it would be together or apart remained to be seen.

Mason decided to take a hot shower. Hopefully it would relax him enough to sleep. He would spend the next day in New York to clear his head, sample some of the city's finest cuisine, and to get the kids some souvenirs. His mind was made up, and he was at peace with his decision.

The next afternoon, Lillian's eyes were still full of tears as she sat on the sofa, watching TV. She hadn't heard from Mason, so she drowned her sorrows in a container of homemade vanilla ice cream covered with chocolate syrup. She was lonely, hurt, and bitter, and drowning her misery in a high-calorie treat usually made her feel better, but for some reason, this time, it wasn't working. Her heart was broken, and she ached for Mason. The last few days they had spent together had been wonderful, and now she was full of regrets.

"Where are you, Mason?" she mumbled to herself as she set the container on the table and wiped her eyes. "I'm sorry, baby. I'm going to make it up to you. You'll see."

She picked up her cell phone to see if she had a missed call, and then walked over to the window. She dialed Mason's number and prayed that he would answer.

"Come on, baby, pick up the phone," she pleaded. After four rings, it went into his voicemail.

"Mason, sweetheart, it's Lillian. Listen, I know things got a little out of hand between us, and we both said a lot of things we didn't mean. I love you. Please call me back. We have a lot of unfinished business to settle, and I promise I won't make you angry. I love you. Call me."

She hung up the cell phone and dropped to her knees and sobbed once again. Mason was the love of her life, and if she had ruined the chance for them to get back together, she would never forgive herself. She was a D.A., and she had to start thinking like one, so she regrouped and decided to call the D.C. hotel where he had checked in, to see if he was still there.

The hotel's policy was not to give out any information on their guests. Lillian cursed out the hotel employee and threw her cell phone on the sofa. She stormed into her bedroom, slammed her face repeatedly into her bedroom door, and then ransacked the living room and the bedroom. Next, she took several pictures of her face and sent the pictures and a questionable text to her lover. She knew it would only be a matter of time before he called back, and she was right.

"What's going on, Lillian? Why did you send me those pictures?" Mason asked.

"Don't you remember? You beat me up," Lillian chastised him.

"I didn't touch you, you crazy-ass bitch!" he yelled at her through the cell phone. "I don't know what's wrong with you, but you need help!"

"No! What I need is for you to get back over to my house, and if you don't, I'll be calling 911."

Mason couldn't believe his ears or eyes as he glanced down at the pictures on his cell phone. "If you want to call the police, go ahead. I'm not coming back over to your house."

Lillian ran her hand through her hair with frustration. Mason wasn't falling for her scheme, but she had gone too far to give up now.

"Why are you doing this to me, Mason? We had such a good time the last few days."

"Listen, Lillian, I'm done," he announced. "I'll admit that

I've made some mistakes this week, and I let our past interfere with the present, but I'm serious when I say it's over. If I'm the father of your daughter, I'll take care of my responsibility, but I will not let you control my life."

"Who do you think you are?" she asked angrily. "I know you don't think you're going to send me a check every week and think your job is done. Hell no! You will be in your daughter's life whether you like it or not."

Mason said, "Get a lawyer, Lillian, because I don't want to have anything else to do with you."

"So, you're not coming back over to my house?" she asked.

Aggravated, Mason yelled, "I'm not in D.C., Lillian, and even if I was, I wouldn't come back to your house! Get some help for your daughter's sake."

"You can go to hell, you son of a bitch!" she yelled into the telephone before hanging up.

Mason looked at his watch and hurried back to his hotel so he could check out and get to the airport. He had purchased all the souvenirs he wanted for his family, and ate lunch at Sylvia's, a famous restaurant in Harlem. Now all he wanted to do was get back to Atlanta as fast as possible. He realized he had a battle ahead of him with Lillian. He just prayed his marriage would be able to sustain another blow to its already fragile state.

Since Mason's hotel was near the airport, it didn't take him long to get there on the hotel shuttle. Before boarding his flight, he placed a call to his brother.

"Vincent, it's Mason. I'm getting ready to board my flight. Can you pick me up at the airport around seven P.M.?"

***

Vincent looked across his desk at his secretary and dismissed her so he could talk to his brother in private.

"I can pick you up. How did things go with Lillian? Did you get the tests?"

Mason sighed and said, "No, and everything's gone to hell, bro. Lillian has some serious issues."

"What happened?" Vincent asked. "I thought you said she wouldn't give you any more trouble and that you had her under control."

"I was wrong," he answered. "Listen, I'm boarding. I can't talk about it right now, but I'll explain everything to you when I see you."

"Does C. J. know you're headed home?" Vincent asked curiously.

"I don't have time to call her. You can let her know if you want to; otherwise, I'll call her once I land."

"Okay, Mason. Have a safe flight, and I'll see you shortly."

"Thanks, bro," Mason replied before hanging up the telephone and boarding the plane.

Later that night, Vincent met his brother at the airport. He noticed the stress in his eyes as they waited in the baggage area for his suitcase.

"Thanks for picking me up, Vincent."

"It was no big deal. I'm glad you made it back safely."

"Me too," he answered. "Did you get in touch with Cherise?"

"I tried, but it went into voicemail, so I sent her a text. Her receptionist said she was out on a scene and would probably be tied up for a few more hours."

The turnstile began to circulate, and suitcase after suitcase appeared on the belt. Mason was happy to see that his luggage was in the first group coming down the turnstile.

Mason quickly grabbed his bag and nervously asked, "Are the kids at home?"

"I don't know where they are, Mason, but if they're not home, they're probably at Patrice's," Vincent pointed out. "What's wrong? And don't tell me nothing, because you're acting weird."

Mason started walking across the crosswalk toward the parking garage. When they reached Vincent's car, he said, "I need to talk to Lorenzo Barnes."

"Why do you need to talk to Lorenzo?" Vincent asked, referring to their friend and family attorney.

Mason climbed into the passenger's seat and said, "I screwed up big time, bro. I let Lillian get back in my system. That woman really is crazy."

"What did you do?"

That's when Mason passed his cell phone over to Vincent so he could see the pictures Lillian had sent him.

Shocked, Vincent asked, "Did you do that to her?"

"No! I didn't touch her. I don't know how her face got bruised like that, but she's threatening to say I did it if I don't come back to her house."

"Did you sleep with her?" Vincent asked, already sensing the answer.

Mason, embarrassed to admit his infidelity, had no choice but to come clean with his brother. "Yeah," he reluctantly admitted. "I don't know what happens to me when I'm around her. She has this strange hold over me."

"That's bullshit and you know it!" Vincent yelled at Mason. "It's not like she put a goddamn gun to your head."

"The woman is beautiful, intelligent—"

Vincent cut him off and said, "Let you tell it, they were all beautiful, but the fact remains that you can't seem to control your thirst for other women."

Mason nodded in agreement and said, "You're right, and the bad thing is that I think Lillian's having some mental issues."

"You're the one with mental issues, bro. Why in the hell would you . . . You know what, Mason? You have the best . . . Forget it. I'm wasting my breath talking to you."

Mason studied Vincent and could see the vein in his forehead pulsing.

"Say it," Mason urged him.

"Say what?" Vincent asked.

Mason laughed and said, "The gloves are off. Go ahead and say what's on your mind."

Vincent was clearly irate. He looked over at Mason and thought, *What the hell?* He was tired of holding back his feelings.

"What's on my mind is how you could ever question how Cherise ended up in my bed." Mason frowned and asked, "What the hell are you saying?"

Vincent hesitated. Here Mason was, married to the woman who was supposed to be the love of *his life,* and all he'd done was emotionally abuse her with his lack of respect for his marriage.

"I'm not saying anything you don't already know," Vincent explained.

"Cherise is not like the average woman. She deals with death each and every day, and that affects her state of mind and emotions. If you truly love her, she'll give it back to you in return, but you can't seem to do that, so it's not hard for her to be drawn elsewhere, especially when you're cheating on her."

"You son of a bitch," Mason mumbled.

"Maybe so, but you're one too," Vincent yelled. "Can you honestly compare what C. J. did with me to what you did? How many were there?"

"Go to hell, Vincent. You don't think I'm blind, do you?" he yelled. "I see the way you look at her and the way she looks at you."

"I never meant to hurt you, bro. I tried to tell you years ago to cut down on the undercover work. Your wife and your children needed you home a lot more than you wanted to be there. You had a choice."

He turned away from Vincent and closed his eyes. "I tried; I really did. You know what it's like being a cop—women, drugs, money, women. I was only trying to provide for my family."

Mason's statement about drugs surprised Vincent. Concerned, he asked, "Are you on drugs, Mason?"

He lowered his head and said, "I do a little coke from time to time, just to take the edge off. It's nothing serious."

"You have got to be kidding me. You're a cop," Vincent reminded him. "You're doing drugs? You're going to lose your job and your pension."

"I love her, Vincent."

"I know you do, but so do I," he admitted. "I love you too. That's why you need to take a leave of absence and get yourself cleaned up. If your drug use and your affair with Lillian, along with an illegitimate child, get out in the press, you're done. I'm going to help you, Mason, but you have to agree to get help for the drugs and your infidelity. Now, tell me if you put your hands on Lillian so I can help you get out of this mess."

"All I did was push her on the floor so I could get out

of there," Mason said as he looked down at the cell phone. "She's trying to set me up."

Vincent sped down the interstate. He had the answer to one question, but he needed more.

"What about the drugs? Do you have any in the house, or on you now?"

"I told you, I only do it from time to time when I'm stressed," Mason explained. "I would never keep it in the house."

"You're going to have a lot of explaining to do if that woman takes those pictures to the police. You were there, and I'm sure some of her neighbors saw you there. It's going to be a hard charge to defend if she brings them against you."

Mason looked out the window and said, "I'm living in my own nightmare."

"Only if you let it be," Vincent replied.

Mason turned to his brother and said, "I'm being blackmailed by a woman I used to care about and who could possibly be the mother of my child, and my wife is in love with my brother. What do you call it?"

"Consequences," Vincent answered casually.

"Just take me home," Mason responded as he pushed the seat back and closed his eyes. The truth was out, and the pain was excruciating. He was in a place he never thought he would be, and he was going to need Vincent's help whether he wanted it or not.

The rest of the ride was somewhat quiet. Vincent could tell that his brother was in deep thought over the predicament he was in as a result of his reckless behavior. Things had gone from bad to worse, and where things would end up was anybody's guess.

Several minutes later, Vincent pulled into Mason's driveway and shut off the engine. He popped the trunk, and they both climbed out of the car.

Mason pulled his suitcase out of the trunk and said, "I'm going to get help."

"I hope so," Vincent replied as he closed the trunk. "Are we good?"

"Do I have a choice?" Mason asked as he walked around to the driver's side of the car.

"You always have a choice, Mason. We've both made mistakes. Right now, all I care about is you getting the help you need and that your family is happy. You can deal with me and my relationship with Cherise any time you want to. I feel bad about it, but it doesn't change the way I feel about her. If you want to settle this now, we can."

Mason set his suitcase on the ground and asked, "What do you expect me to do? The night you told me about your affair with Cherise, I wanted to kill you, but because of my own guilt, all I could do was hit you."

Vincent rubbed his cheek and said, "I remember."

"It didn't matter that I was sleeping with Vada at the time, as well as a couple of other women. I trusted you."

"I know you did, and I'm sorry it happened, but it really wasn't about me. C. J. trusted you too, but after the third affair, and then Vada, she was done."

Vada and her brother were the target of Mason's undercover sting. He infiltrated the drug ring as her boyfriend so he could bring down her brother's drug operation. Little did he know how far his role of boyfriend would go, but he played the role great, maybe even a little too good, causing Vada to fall in love with him. When his cover was blown, she felt betrayed, and she sought revenge.

Mason picked up his suitcase and walked down the sidewalk in silence. It still hurt to visualize his brother making love to Cherise. It was an image he was sure his wife had played over and over in her head each time she found out about his many affairs.

"I don't want to talk about it anymore, Vincent," Mason said as he made his way up on the porch.

"When are you going to call Lorenzo?"

"As soon as I can," he answered.

Frustrated, Vincent followed Mason into the house and watched him deactivate the alarm.

"What set Lillian off?" Vincent asked.

Mason set his suitcase in the hallway and said, "All I did was tell her I wasn't leaving Cherise over her daughter."

"The last time I talked to you, you acted as if you had everything under control, and you didn't mention anything about sleeping with her."

Mason leaned against the wall and said, "She started kissing me, talking about how no one would ever know, and that she still loved me. Then she took my hand and made me touch her," he explained. "I pretty much lost it after that. She felt like a wildfire raging over me."

Vincent shook his head and asked, "Do you have any idea how much this is going to cost you? And I'm not talking about just the money. Was it worth it?"

"No amount of money is worth me losing Cherise and the kids," he responded in a daze as he thumbed through the stack of mail on the hallway table.

"If that child is yours, or she has you charged with assault, she's going to take you to the cleaners."

Mason turned on the television and said, "I made a mistake, and I'm sick over this. Right now, all I want to do is kiss my wife and kids and forget about Lillian."

Before Vincent could respond, Janelle sprinted into the room and jumped into her father's arms. "Daddy! You're home!"

Vincent seemed to be started by Janelle as she bolted into the room. They were so deep in conversation that they didn't even hear the garage door go up.

"I am, and I brought you a Yankees baseball hat," he replied as he walked over to his carry-on bag and pulled out the hat. He put it on her head and gave her a kiss.

"Sweetheart, I missed you guys so much."

Janelle held on to her father's neck as she smiled and waved at her uncle.

"Hello, Janelle," Vincent answered before turning to Mase, who had entered the room.

"Hey, Unc," Mase greeted with a brotherly handshake.

Mase made his way over to his father and hugged him as well. "Hey, Dad. Welcome back."

Mason hugged his son and then congratulated him on winning his last ballgame. He handed his son a New York Knicks basketball jersey, putting a huge smile on his son's face.

"Thanks, Dad," Mase said with appreciation. As he headed out of the room, he bumped fists with Vincent and then ran upstairs to his room, with Janelle close behind.

"I see everybody's here," Cherise pointed out as she entered the room and set her purse on the table. "Why didn't you call to let me know you were coming back? We could've picked you up from the airport so Vincent wouldn't have to go out of his way."

Without answering, he pulled her into his arms for a long, loving hug and kiss. "I missed you."

Cherise glanced over at Vincent and said, "Hey, brother-in-law. What's up? You look stressed."

"It goes with the territory," he remarked before giving her a kiss on the cheek. "You look beautiful as always."

"Thank you, Vincent."

"You're welcome," he replied before giving Mason a hug. It was a hug he needed to give his brother because he knew their relationship would never be the same after he'd reaffirmed his love for Cherise to his brother.

"I'm getting ready to go. I love you, Mason," he announced. "Handle your business, and call me later if you want to talk."

Mason accepted his brother's hug because he knew if anybody was going to help him get out of this mess with Lillian, it would be Vincent. He was a loyal officer of the law, but if he had to get down and dirty to protect his family, he could and would.

"I love you too, bro," Mason replied as he possessively held on to Cherise's waist.

Vincent stepped back and asked, "Are we good?"

"Consequences, remember? We're good."

Cherise tilted her head and observed the two men. She wasn't sure what was going on between them, but whatever it was, must be serious. She just hoped it wasn't what she thought it was. It was her responsibility to tell Mason about her relationship with Vincent, not his.

Vincent looked into her eyes and said, "Good night, C. J."

The soothing tone of his voice sent a warm sensation over her body, and it aroused her in the presence of her husband.

"Good night, Vincent."

Mason released her long enough to walk Vincent out to his car, where he thanked him for his confidentiality, advice, and brotherly love—then forgave him.

When he reentered the house, Cherise was upstairs reminding the kids about their daily chores before bedtime. As she exited Janelle's room, she met Mason at the top of the stairs with his suitcase. He locked eyes with her and smiled as he followed her into their bedroom.

"Do you have any clothes to send to the cleaners?" she asked as she removed her shoes.

"I do, but I'll drop them off when I go into the office in the morning," he answered as he set the suitcase on the floor. The last thing he needed was her seeing any signs of Lillian's lipstick on his clothing before he could rid himself of her threat. Women were very observant and had a keen sense of smell when it came to another woman.

"Okay. I'm getting ready to shower and crash. I'm glad you made it home safely. It's been a crazy few days at work," she revealed. "Hopefully, I'll have more energy tomorrow to stay up and talk to you about your trip."

"Cool," he answered before following her into the bathroom, where he watched her undress down to her bra and panties. She was absolutely beautiful, and once again, he was reminded just how much of a fool he'd been.

He pulled her into his arms, and cupped her face so he could look her in the eyes. "You know I love you, right?"

She forced a smile and said, "Yeah, I know."

He kissed her once more, and then patted her lovingly on her backside. "Get some rest. I'm going to spend some time with the kids before turning in myself, but before I do, I have two tickets to see *The Color Purple* for next month. It's just you and me, baby, out on the town in the Big Apple. What do you say?"

"It sounds nice, babe, but I'll have to check my calendar."

"I know, but we need a chance to get away, just the two of us."

She turned on the shower and turned her back to him. "I'll let you know, Mason."

"That's cool," he said before closing the bathroom door. As he leaned against it, he was a little shaken by Cherise's obvious distance. Could she already know about Lillian?

He moved away from the door and looked around the bedroom. He actually had the perfect life and family, and he'd been stupid to gamble it all on Lillian.

Chapter Sixteen

The next morning, Vincent yawned as he entered his office. He'd had a restless night after confessing to his brother. He knew he wouldn't be able to concentrate on work. Most men in his position would seize the opportunity to swoop in on Cherise, but he couldn't, no matter how much he loved her. He felt like his duty at the moment was to help his brother.

The first order of business was to call their attorney to find out if Mason had talked to him. Second order of business was to make a call to the district attorney's office in D.C. to try to talk some sense into Lillian. He wasn't sure if she would be in, since her face was covered in bruises. He needed to find out her motives and try to resolve the problem. If she wouldn't listen to reason, he would move on to his third order of business, which was to make her an offer she couldn't refuse.

He was on a mission, so he asked his secretary to hold his calls and postpone his meetings until the afternoon. He dialed Lorenzo's number, but his cell phone went to voicemail, so he called his office and found out he would be in court all morning.

Vincent hung up the telephone and placed his second call to the D.C. district attorney's office. He identified himself to the receptionist, and after being transferred a couple of times, he landed in the office of the assistant district attorney. Vincent didn't want to reveal his real reason for contacting the office; instead, he fabricated a story that he needed to talk with Lillian regarding a case she prosecuted when she was with the district attorney's office in Atlanta. The court officer hesitated for a moment and then put him on hold for what seemed like forever. When the assistant returned to the telephone, she told Vincent that Lillian no longer worked for the D.A.'s office and, in fact, had been gone for several years. When Vincent pushed for more information, the lady informed him that due to Lillian's privacy and the safety of the court officers, she wasn't at liberty to reveal any more information.

Vincent thanked her for the information and hung up more puzzled than before he called. If Lillian wasn't working for the D.A.'s office, he now wondered what she was doing. She could be in private practice, not uncommon for most lawyers. He was intrigued, but his ringing cell phone made him put his investigation on hold until later.

"Vincent, we need to talk . . . now," Cherise said on the other end of the phone.

"I can't right now. I'm really tied up with something."

She sighed and said, "Well, you're going to have to untie yourself, because we have to talk. Meet me at the gazebo in Piedmont Park in twenty minutes."

"Okay," he answered as he quickly hit the print button on his laptop.

Minutes later, Vincent found Cherise pacing back and forth in front of the gazebo. Before he could ask her what was wrong, she shoved her cell phone in his face and showed him a series of pictures sent to her on her cell phone.

"Is this who I think it is?" she asked angrily. "Don't lie, because I know you know."

Vincent slowly took her phone out of her hand and looked at picture after picture of Mason, naked and asleep. Another picture was of a naked Lillian snuggled up to Mason with a big smile on her face. There were others of his body, showing various tattoos, leaving no possibility for him to deny anything.

"Damn," he mumbled.

"Is that all you can say?" she yelled at her brother-in-law.

The pictures had him momentarily in shock. "Where did you get these?"

"They came in from a private number," she revealed. "I'm sure that bitch sent them to me. I knew something was going on. I just didn't know what. He's been acting strange for a while. You knew, didn't you?"

He looked away, not wanting to make eye contact with her. "You really need to talk to Mason."

She put her hands over her eyes and said, "God! I've been such a fool! I've been so worried about breaking his heart, and he's laid up with this whore. But it's okay. I know what I need to do."

He grabbed her arm and asked, "What do you mean?"

She pulled her arm away from him and said, "You're not in this, remember?"

Their altercation caught the eye of two ladies jogging by, but they continued on with their jog.

"You know what I meant," he replied.

"I feel so stupid! It's obvious he can't stay away from her, so you know what? They can have each other. Now I realize that she was the one behind the text messages and vandalizing my car."

"This situation is a little more complicated, C. J."

She shoved her cell phone back in his face and said, "Does

this look complicated to you? What do you know, Vincent?"

"It's not my place to say. You need to call Mason so you guys can talk."

"There's nothing to talk about. Here I was all worried about breaking his heart, and for what? He can't apologize his way out of this one. This is the last time he's going to flaunt his affairs in my face. I'll make sure of that."

Cherise was beyond angry. She was so angry he couldn't tell if she was she talking about harming Mason or just ending the marriage. Either way, he could see the vein in her neck pulsating, and her eyes were red and full of tears.

"You need to calm down and think before you act. You said yourself that you had to think about the kids when you were ready to tell Mason about us. Don't be so quick to put this situation on blast with the kids. It's going to affect them," he responded.

"What's really going on, Vincent?" she asked. "I thought you were ready to tell Mason about us too. Why are you so concerned about him now?"

"I told you, it's complicated. He has some issues he's trying to resolve with this woman, and if you confront him with this now, it's going to mess everything up."

She walked over to her brother-in-law and asked, "Do you honestly think I care anymore? Mason helped turn me into someone I never thought I would be."

Vincent took her by the hand and said, "I didn't help the situation. I knew you were vulnerable at the time. I'm just as much at fault."

She touched his face lovingly. "Vincent, I don't regret loving you, but I do regret making a bad situation worse by falling in love with you."

"Give yourself some credit," he acknowledged. "You did try to make your marriage work."

"I feel like it was all a waste of time," she admitted. "I don't think Mason was as serious as I was."

"What now?" he asked.

"I've come to realize that I've been trying to hold on to something that's been over for a long time. Mason wasn't ready for the responsibility of a wife and family. He was an undercover cop. That was the life he loved, and he couldn't truly love both at the same time."

"That's not true," Vincent added. "He does love you."

She looked down at the pictures on her cell phone and said, "He has a funny way of showing it."

Cherise and Mason had their ups and downs during their young marriage. Mason got a rush from his undercover work, and it made him feel invincible, but instead of sharing his successes with his wife, he fell into the lion's den with Lillian. He felt as though Lillian, as a prosecutor, understood what he was dealing with on the streets, so he excluded Cherise from the sordid details, even though she was in the trenches with him investigating horrific crimes as a crime scene investigator. Mason got it twisted, and now it was going to take a miracle to save him.

Vincent stroked Cherise's trembling hand. Her pain was visible, and he wanted so badly to take it away. If he could get her in the car and just drive, maybe her anger would subside so she could think more clearly about her approach to Mason.

"I have to go," she announced as she started walking toward the parking lot.

He grabbed her arm once again and said, "You don't need to drive in this condition. You're pissed, and I'm afraid you're going to hurt yourself or somebody else."

"I'm fine," she answered. "Mason's the one you need to worry about."

Her demeanor was all over the place, angry one minute, calm the next, and it unnerved him. She was unstable and he knew it. He also knew she had a permit to carry a sidearm, and he had concerns about what she might do with it if he allowed her to leave.

"You're not leaving here alone. You're riding with me," he demanded.

She was emotionally exhausted and couldn't talk about it anymore. As they walked to his car, she erupted in tears, and her legs became weak. He wrapped his arm around her waist and steadied her until they made it back to his car. He opened the passenger's side door for her.

Before taking a seat, she asked, "What about my truck?"

"I got it," he answered.

Vincent closed her door and pulled out his cell phone to call Mason. As usual, he got his voicemail, causing him to curse out loud. He needed to tell his brother about the pictures as soon as possible. Before entering the car, he tried calling him again, but it went into his voice mail.

"Do you need me to call your office for you?" Vincent asked after joining her in the car.

At this point, she was sobbing uncontrollably. He opened his glove compartment and pulled out a box of tissue and handed it to her.

"I'm off today," she answered softly before blowing her nose.

It tore at his heart to see Cherise so distraught, but he'd seen her in this condition before, and sadly, it was for similar reasons. His mind was racing, and so was his heart, because he knew he had to locate his brother and fast.

"Where's your gun?" Vincent asked Cherise.

She wiped her eyes and said, "In my purse."

He held his hand out to her and said, "Give it to me."

Without hesitation, she reached inside her purse and handed him the firearm. He knew her very well, and it wasn't like she hadn't threatened Lillian with a gun before. This time, he was concerned she just might use it on Mason, and he couldn't let that happen.

"I know you're upset, and you have every right to be, but if you're thinking about doing something to my brother, you need to get that out of your head. I told him to get help for his issues, but he said he had everything under control."

Vincent pulled out of the park and decided to drive until he got in touch with Mason. As he drove, Cherise seemed to calm down a little bit.

"I want you to know that I would never try to take Mason's life, especially over a woman. Yes, I'm pissed and hurt, so of course I have crazy thoughts floating around in my head, but he's the father of my children."

Vincent looked over at her and said, "I hear you, but he's my brother and I'm a cop. I have to be sure."

Mason was running late to get to the office. As he hurried down the stairs, he turned on his cell phone and saw that he had several missed calls and text messages. The first text was the same pictures Lillian had sent to Cherise. Accompanying the pictures was the message: I TOLD YOU YOU WOULD BE SORRY.

He had to grab the stair rail because he nearly missed the last step after viewing the pictures. Once again, he was reminded of the position he'd put himself in. He had been totally unaware that she had taken the pictures. Livid, he immediately called Lillian's number and paced the floor as he waited for her to answer. It didn't take but two rings before she answered, and the first thing he heard was laughter.

"Did you like the pictures, baby?" she asked as she continued to laugh.

"What the hell is wrong with you?" he asked as he sat down at the kitchen table. "Why would you take pictures like that?"

"I thought you might want a little reminder of our time together."

Mason couldn't think straight. His head was pounding, and he realized the situation with Lillian was beyond the point of no return. She was totally out of control.

"Why can't you just leave it alone?" Mason asked. "I made a mistake sleeping with you again. It's over."

Lillian laughed again, and then anger set in. "It's not over until I say it's over. Baby, this is just the beginning. You'll see."

Before he could respond, she hung up the telephone.

Mason couldn't move. He had no idea what Lillian's threat meant, but he knew whatever it was, it wouldn't be good.

While he was sitting there, he decided to check his other messages. He had missed calls from Vincent, and a text message from Janelle, with her usual I LOVE YOU message. With all the madness going on with Lillian, those three words from his daughter seemed to make all the drama with Lillian a distant memory. It put a smile on his face, but the smile didn't last long. Before he could get out the door, his cell phone rang.

"Mason, where are you?"

He let out a loud sigh and said, "I'm getting ready to leave the house. What's up?"

"There's a problem. Lillian sent Cherise pictures of the two of you together and she's pissed."

Now Mason knew what Lillian meant when she indicated that it wasn't over. She obviously used her connections to get Cherise's cell phone number. Now he had to go in damage control mode.

He felt lightheaded as he leaned against the door. "Where is she?"

"With me," he answered. "Don't leave. I'm bringing her home so you guys can talk."

Thirty-five minutes later, Vincent pulled into the driveway and shut off his engine. He looked over at Cherise and asked, "Are you going to be okay?"

She opened the car door and said, "I'll never be okay."

He climbed out of the car and waited for her as she walked around the car. He didn't know what to expect when they got inside, but he had a bad feeling about the whole meeting. He understood that none of their lives would ever be the same. What he didn't know was how different their lives would be at the rising of the morning sun.

Chapter Seventeen

Cherise unlocked the front door and entered, with Vincent following closely behind. She turned to him and asked "What about my truck?"

"I told you I got it. A cab's on the way to pick me up so I can drive it back to the house for you."

"Thank you," she replied as she handed him her keys. They walked into the family room and found Mason sitting on the sofa with his head in his hands. He looked up at her with tears in his eyes and shook his head with despair. Cherise set her purse on the chair and stood in front of Mason with her arms folded. He looked so broken and sad, but Cherise's anger had returned, and it was clearly visible.

Vincent looked over at his brother and said, "Look, I know you guys have a lot to talk about. I'm getting ready to go pick up C. J.'s truck, but I can't go unless I know you two are going to be cool."

Neither of them responded as they continued to stare into each other's eyes. That's when Vincent remembered that Mason still had his gun. He walked over to his brother and held out his hand.

"Give me your gun, bro."

"My gun?" he asked. "Why do you need my gun?"

"Because I said so," he replied. "I took C. J.'s from her, and I'm taking yours too. I'm not taking any chances. Now, give me the gun."

Mason pulled his gun out of his shoulder hoister and hand-ed it his brother.

"Thank you," he replied before exiting the room and the house, leaving Cherise and Mason alone. Vincent put Ma-son's weapon in the trunk of his car just as the cab driver pulled up. He climbed inside the vehicle, hoping the couple would come to some type of solution for their marriage once and for all.

"Where to?" the cab driver asked as he pulled away from the curb.

"Piedmont Park," Vincent answered as he pulled out his BlackBerry and started doing his own detective work. He did a Google search on Lillian to see if he could find more in-formation on why she no longer worked in the D.A.'s office. Several articles popped up immediately, but there was one article in particular that nearly knocked him out.

Assistant District Attorney Lillian Green hospitalized after having a mental breakdown during the trial of accused husband-murderer Madeline Vanoir. Ms. Green was in the process of cross examining Mrs. Vanoir about her infidelities when she ignored Judge Payne's repeated out of order pleas, leaving him no choice but to hold her in contempt of court.

Lillian Green, who's spent four years in the D.A.'s office, sobbed and babbled uncontrollably as she was physically removed from the courtroom by court officers. Sources revealed under the con-dition of anonymity that Ms. Green, a single mother, had been under tremendous stress since a family tragedy months earlier.

A spokesman from the district attorney's office refused to com-ment on camera, or release the details of Ms. Green's situation, but stated that they were saddened over the court appearance. They went on to say that she had been a tough prosecutor and

well-respected attorney, and has had difficulty coping with her family tragedy. The district attorney's office does not hold Ms. Green responsible for her actions, and wishes her a speedy recovery.

   Judge Payne threw out her contempt of court charge and ordered the D.A.'s office to replace Ms. Green immediately.

"What the hell?" Vincent mumbled as he quickly sent Mason a text.

Cherise took her cell phone out of her purse, pulled up the pictures Lillian sent, and set it in front of Mason.

He looked down at the pictures and said, "Baby, I'm sorry."

"Mason, you sound like a broken record. How many times have you had to say that to me?"

Mason took a breath and said, "I didn't plan for that to happen. I haven't seen Lillian in years."

Cherise glanced down at the pictures and sarcastically said, "You didn't seem to have a hard time picking up where you left off. You didn't have to lie about going to New York. Why do you have such a hard time telling me the truth?"

"I didn't want to hurt you, Cherise, and whether you want to believe me or not, I didn't go to D.C. to be with her. It was business, and things just got out of hand."

She crossed her legs and said, "That's an understatement."

Mason paced the floor and tried to find the words to explain his situation with Lillian. He decided the best thing was to just tell the truth and let the chips fall where they may.

He took a deep breath and said, "I only went there because Lillian told me I was the father of her daughter. I wanted to get a DNA test done, that's all."

Cherise's heart thumped in her chest. *A daughter?* The news was hitting closer to home than she could ever imagine. How could she condemn Mason when she was in the same situation?

"If that's true, how did you end up in bed with her?"

"I don't know," he admitted. "She started in on me about how much she still loved me, and I wanted to leave, but she started—"

Cherise put her hand up to stop him. She didn't need to hear the details. The pictures spoke for themselves, and there was nothing left to the imagination.

"Do you love her?"

"I care about her, but it's you I love," he answered.

Cherise briefly closed her eyes and then asked, "Are you in love with me, Mason?"

He hesitated for a second and answered, "You're my wife. How can you ask me some bull like that?"

"I was your wife the first time you had an affair with her, as well as all the others. I need to know, Mason. Are you in love with me?" she asked again.

"You're my wife!" he responded in anger and confusion. "I made a mistake! All I need to know right now is if you can forgive me and support me while I find out if I'm the father of her daughter. Lillian has some issues, and if that child is my daughter, I can't have the child living with her mother. She's unstable."

Cherise jumped in Mason's face and yelled, "Who in the hell do you think you're talking to? You promised me, Mason!"

He grabbed her wrists to try to calm her down. "Cherise, I know what I did was unforgivable, and I have no excuse for what I did. I don't want to lose you."

Tears fell out of her eyes. "This marriage has been on life support for a long time. It's time we stop trying make it work and just let it go. It's suffered too much damage."

He stared at her and saw the seriousness in her eyes. Yes, he'd screwed up, but he didn't want a divorce, or for his children to grow up in a broken home.

"We can get past this, baby. Think about the children."

"Don't you dare try to use the children as leverage. You weren't thinking about the children when you were rolling around in bed with that woman. "You're not in love with me, Mason. Admit it. And as painful as it is to say it, I haven't felt real love between us in a while. I thought we had another chance after the shooting, but you and I both know we were fooling ourselves. I love you with all my heart, and I'll always love you, but I can't trust you anymore. We're not happy, and we're not in love."

Mason walked over to Cherise and pulled her into his arms. He hugged her tightly and whispered, "I do love you, Cherise. Please, give me a chance to make it up to you."

She stepped out of his embrace and pointed to her chest. Tears fell out of her eyes and with her voice cracking, she replied, "I can't, Mason. My heart is shattered."

Mason shoved his hands in his pockets and walked over to the window. "I gave you another chance when I found out about you and my brother."

She didn't expect him to go there, but he had, and their conversation had gone to another level.

Mason turned to his wife, and with a straight face, said, "I know about you and Vincent."

Cherise was stunned. She wasn't expecting to talk about her relationship with Vincent until later.

"What is it that you think you know?" she asked.

"Come on, Cherise. I'm not stupid. I know I put that into motion, and I have to live with what happened. But even though I was with Lillian, never once did I think you and my brother would hook up."

"Do you think it's something I planned?" Cherise asked in defense.

"I don't know what to think, sweetheart. All I know is somewhere along the line we lost our connection, and for some reason, I felt like Lillian understood me better. What happened to us, Cherise?"

She walked over to the window and stood next to him. "Life happened to us. I think we're both guilty of sabotaging our marriage. It's not like the love was never there. My heart still flutters when you look at me that certain way."

He smiled and said, "I know exactly what you mean. Can you ever forgive me?"

Cherise, filled with her own guilt, wrapped her arms around Mason's neck and said, "As long as you can forgive me too. I love you, Mason, and you'll always have a special place in my heart."

Their situations were no different, and she realized there was no way she could reveal that Janelle was not his daughter. It would devastate him much worse than the breakup of their marriage.

"I love you too, and I would appreciate it if you could hold off on telling the children about this. I need to get this thing settled with Lillian."

Cherise pulled a tissue out of a box and wiped her eyes before hugging his neck. "I'm sorry, Mason."

"I'm sorry too, baby."

"How old is the little girl?"

Mason filled Cherise in on what he knew about Lillian's daughter. As he spoke, she could hear the pain in his voice and the tone of defeat. She wanted to reassure him that she did love him, and she felt the need to do something to re-deem herself from her own indiscretions.

Surprisingly, she asked, "Is there anything I can do to help? I know it has to be weighing on your mind."

"I don't have a right to ask you for help."

"You didn't ask. I offered," she responded. "It's the least I can do under the circumstances. We're still family, Mason, and family sticks up for each other no matter what."

Cherise's offer warmed his heart. There was no way he could refuse her help if it meant protecting his family and saving his career. He smiled, but was then distracted when his cell phone buzzed.

"Is that her?" Cherise asked curiously.

Mason picked up his cell phone and read his text message. "No, it's from Vincent."

Cherise watched Mason's facial expressions as he read Vincent's message about the article he found online.

"What is it?" Cherise asked.

He handed his cell phone to his wife so she could read the text, and he left the room. It was all clear to him now. Lillian was unstable, and more seriously, unpredictable. Most puzzling was the nature of the tragedy the article spoke of, which could establish the foundation for her unstable behavior once and for all.

He couldn't deal with it right now. His hands were full with his troubled marriage. Hopefully, Vincent could find out more information so Lillian could get the help she so desperately needed.

Lillian sat across from the detective and started giving him her statement. Her bruises were still well defined. She had a black eye, and the corner of her lip was swollen.

"So, you're saying the man who attacked you is your ex-lover and a police officer?"

"Yes, he's a cold case detective, but he used to work undercover. He's very dangerous."

All Lillian wanted to do was get Mason back to D.C., on her turf, and she would drop the assault charges. She was holding his career in the palm of her hand, and she knew he would protect it at any cost.

The detective jotted down the information and then leaned back in his chair. "Miss Green, do you know why Detective McKenzie attacked you?"

Lillian crossed her legs and said, "Mason McKenzie's married. The only answer I have is that he came here to try to rekindle our relationship. When I told him I wasn't going to be his little mistress anymore, he went into a rage."

The detective turned to his computer and typed in Mason's name. What came up showed nothing in Mason's background, other than him being a stellar officer and decorated detective. He'd won all sorts of commendations and awards, making it hard to believe that he had brutalized Lillian.

He turned back to Lillian and asked, "Once I issue an arrest warrant, there's no turning back. Are you ready to take this all the way?"

Lillian stood and pulled her purse up on her shoulder. "I didn't stutter. I want him picked up and charged. If you can't do the job, I'll find somebody else who can. I know how you cops are. You stick up for each other no matter what, but I'm not letting him get away with this. He screwed with the wrong woman, and I want his ass back in D.C. to answer to me."

The detective also stood upon hearing Lillian's threats. It made him angry that she was insinuating that he might not do his job. He grabbed the statement she had given him and firmly said, "Ma'am, I can assure you I know how to do my job. We take every complaint seriously and investigate them thoroughly. I'll be in touch with you about our progress in this case."

"You'd better, or I'll be back to talk to your lieutenant, and I won't be so nice."

Before the detective could respond, Lillian quickly walked out of the office and into the elevator.

Pissed off, the detective took Lillian's report and slid it into his desk. He wasn't about to file a report against a fellow officer until he checked into the allegations. Most times, the victim was upset and visibly shaken by her experience. Lillian Green was the total opposite. She was calm, detailed, and very demanding. No tears or emotions, outside of anger. That alone caused him to question the validity of her claim as he picked up the telephone and placed a call to the Atlanta, Georgia Cold Case Division.

He spoke off the record with Mason's lieutenant and a few of his co-workers, and heard nothing but praise for the decorated officer. They couldn't give him an alibi; they informed the detective that Mason had taken a few personal days off during the time Lillian claimed to have been attacked. Before hanging up, he thanked the officers for their time and assured them he was not under investigation. He reminded them that their conversation was off the record, and there was no reason to mention it to Mason.

Lillian sped through the streets of D.C. as her heart pounded in her chest. When she got home, she couldn't remember if all the traffic lights were green or if she was just lucky. In any case, she'd made it home in one piece, and she was even angrier than before she left. The living room still had visible signs of her fight with Mason, and her blood was still on the corner of the bedroom door. She could still smell his cologne—or was it her imagination? In any case, his presence was still very much felt around the house, and it saddened her.

She walked into McKenzie's room and curled up on her bed in the fetal position.

"Mason!" she sobbed hysterically. McKenzie's picture was sitting on the nightstand. She was so pretty. Lillian traced the outline of her daughter's face with her finger, and tears fell down on the glass.

"Momma loves you so much, sweetheart. You look so much like your father. I know he loves you, and don't worry; you're going to love him just as much as I do. Everything's going to be fine. Momma will make sure of that."

Mason and Cherise spent the rest of the afternoon talking until the kids came in from school. They didn't feel ready to tell the children about their divorce, so they decided to try to act as normal as possible. They both felt as if a huge weight had been lifted off their chests, but a different weight was bearing down on them. The anxiety of the children's reaction to their divorce and the results of Mason's DNA test were going to be the last chapters in their story before moving on with their lives.

Their next stop was going to be D.C., but this time, Cherise was going to accompany him. Mason was still her husband, and he wanted her to be by his side for better or worse. It was going to be the first time she had seen Lillian since she had shoved a gun in her face, but this meeting was going to be welcomed, and afterward, Cherise never wanted to see or hear from Lillian Green again.

Their trip was in a week, and before leaving, they wanted

to have some quality family time together, so Mason extended his personal leave, and Cherise took some well-deserved time off. Vincent kept his distance, and continued to investigate Lillian, allowing the couple to work out the details of their marriage.

Mason and Cherise decided to take the kids out on her parents' houseboat for some precious family time. Everything was out in the open now, except the secret surrounding Janelle's paternity. The McKenzies camped out on the shoreline, and did a lot of fishing. The couple knew that once they told the children about their divorce, they would be devastated, so they wanted to make them feel as loved as possible before delivering the terrible news. During the day, they did a lot of fishing, and at night, they played cards and roasted marshmallows over a fire. They were sharing quality family time together, like it should've been, without all the infidelities. Cherise was actually enjoying the closeness of her husband, and he was enjoying hers as well.

One night near midnight, as the couple sat out on the deck of the boat, sipping wine while the children slept, Mason reached over, took Cherise's hand into his, and caressed it lovingly. She smiled as he kissed the back of her hand and wrist.

"I've always loved the feel of your hands. They're so soft, and you have beautiful fingers."

She climbed into the chaise lounge with him and said, "And I've always loved the feel of your lips on my hands. Well, anywhere on my body, as a matter of fact."

Mason chuckled as he wrapped his arms around her body. It was a chilly night on the lake, and the only sounds were their voices and the sounds of wildlife in the forest area lining the cove.

Cherise lay quietly against his chest and listened to the rhythm of his heart. It was mesmerizing, and for that moment, she felt incredibly close to him. It was a feeling she hadn't felt in years.

He took a sip of wine and asked, "Have you told your parents about us yet?"

She sighed and said, "Yes, and they're very upset. Momma said they were disappointed in both of us, and that we should've used better judgment. Daddy was somewhat speechless. He left the room when I told him about me and Vincent. I hurt them so badly. I know the children are going to be just as upset, if not worse. There's going to be a lot that they're not going to understand. I'm so scared."

Mason tilted her chin so he could look into her eyes. He didn't want the night to end with tears, but there was no way around it once the subject had come up.

"The children are stronger than you realize. It's going to hurt them, but I don't plan for them to feel like I'm not in their lives. I want to be a better father for them."

She stood and refilled her glass in silence. Mason helped her back into the chaise lounge.

"Mase saw the text messages from Lillian."

Shocked, Cherise nearly spit out her wine. She coughed a couple of times and then asked, "How?"

"I accidentally left my cell phone at home one day when a text came through."

Angry, Cherise asked, "How could you let that happen?"

"It was an accident," he explained. "He asked me if I was cheating on you. I didn't admit or deny it, but I did tell him there had been some strain in our marriage. He's a smart kid and he loves you. He was not happy with me at all."

"Does he know about me and Vincent?"

"Not that I know of," he replied.

"See, this is exactly what I didn't want to happen. I'm sure he's confused."

"He'll be okay."

"Not Janelle," Cherise responded before draining her glass of wine. "She's a daddy's girl."

"Janelle will adjust, just like she did when I was working undercover. I was gone for weeks at a time, but she never seemed to let it bother her."

"That's because she knew you would eventually be home."

"We'll get through this. We both have to make sure that the children don't feel like they're growing up in a broken home." He kissed her forehead and said, "It's late, and we have a flight to catch tomorrow night. Let's go to bed."

Chapter Eighteen

The day had come for Cherise and Mason to make their way to D.C. After seeing the children off to school, they finished packing their suitcases for what could be an extended trip. While their parents were out of town, the children would be staying with Jonathan and Patricia. They were used to their parents traveling or working extended hours, so staying with their grandparents was second nature.

"Do you think Lillian is going to be upset that I came with you?" Cherise asked as she packed her makeup and other toiletries.

"I don't care. She was wrong for not telling me she had a daughter. This could've been taken care of a long time ago," he replied as he zipped up his suitcase.

Cherise looked over at her husband and sensed his uneasiness. She walked over to him and cupped his face. As she looked into his sad brown eyes, she said, "This whole thing is hard on both of us, but I found a long time ago that the pain doesn't last always, and I want you to know that no matter what, I love you, and I'll always love you. You are a wonderful man, and the best father in the world, so if the little girl is yours, I'll support you, because I know you'll do right by her."

She kissed him lovingly on the lips and he hugged her tight to his body.

"I had a great time on the lake. I'll never forget it for as long as I live," Cherise revealed.

He didn't want to let Cherise go, because he had no idea how many more hugs and kisses he'd be able to get from her.

"It was fun. The kids were so happy."

He backed away from her and said, "I'm so sorry I made such a mess of everything."

She put her finger up to his lips to silence him. "I'm sorry too. I was thoughtless and inconsiderate and should've never given Vincent a second look."

He kissed her cheek and said, "You were sad and alone. If it hadn't been my brother, it would've been someone else. I've forgiven you, you've forgive me, and I know God has forgiven us too. No more apologies. Your happiness and the happiness of my children is all I care about."

She smiled and said, "Me too, sweetheart, me too."

As they traveled together on the last journey of their marriage, they both had made peace with each other. All that was left now was to settle the matter with Lillian so they could move on.

Mason picked up his suitcase and said, "I'm getting ready to take my bags down to the car. I'll be back for yours in a second."

She nodded and went into the bathroom and closet to turn out the lights. When she returned to the bedroom, she heard Mason coming back up the stairs. He seemed to be arguing with someone.

"Mason, who are you talking to?" she called out to him as she stepped out into the hallway. When she turned the corner, she screamed out in disbelief.

Vincent was sitting around the poker table in the home of one of the other Georgia commanders. It was a standing engagement. They usually looked forward to getting together to unwind from their stressful positions, but Vincent's head was not in the game like it normally was. His mind was on Cherise and Mason. He continued to keep his distance, but in fact, he knew they'd been spending some quality time together and that they were going to D.C.

"It's your call, Vincent," one of the commanders called out. He threw his cards down and said, "I'm out."

The commander laughed and said, "I love taking your money."

Vincent turned up his beer and said, "Just remember that payback is hell."

Everyone laughed, but they were interrupted when Vincent's BlackBerry chimed. He stood and said, "Excuse me for second."

"Hello?"

"Is this Vincent McKenzie?" the female caller asked.

"Yes, it is. How may I help you?"

"You left a message on my voicemail asking about my daughter, Lillian. How can I help you?"

Vincent's mood instantly changed as he waved good-bye to his friends and quickly left. Outside the building, Vincent thanked Mrs. Green for returning his call.

"Is my daughter okay? Is she in some kind of trouble?" her mother asked.

"I'm not completely sure, ma'am, but I need you to answer a few questions, if you don't mind."

Vincent slid into his car and started asking Lillian's mother a series of questions regarding Lillian's past and her daughter. The information he received was nothing short of unbelievable, and he ended the call stunned and deeply concerned about Mason and Cherise's trip to D.C.

He looked at his watch and realized that Mason and Cherise should be on their way to the airport. He dialed Mason's number and quickly backed out of his friend's driveway. He couldn't let them get on the plane. If he did, he might never see either one of them again.

Back at the McKenzie house, Cherise screamed as Lillian held the gun on her. "How did you get in here?"

"Don't you worry about it, you bitch!" Lillian yelled at Cherise. "It's because of you that Mason can't seem to make up his mind, but I'm here to help him make up his mind. Ain't that right, baby?"

Cherise looked over at Mason, who had his hands in the air. Lillian had obviously staked out the house and waited for the opportunity to ambush them.

"Lillian, put the gun down before you hurt somebody," Mason pleaded. "This has nothing to do with Cherise. Just let her go."

"I'm not leaving you with this maniac, Mason," Cherise replied.

"Ahhhh, ain't that sweet," Lillian teased. "You're right, Mason. It's not about her, but it is about our daughter," she said as she pulled a picture of her daughter out of her pocket and held it in his face.

"She deserved a father, just like her little bastards!"

"Wait just a damn minute," Mason yelled as he took a step toward her. "You won't talk about my children like that."

"Whatever! I deserved to have you!" she yelled. "You made promises to me, Mason, and you will deliver on them one way or the other. I love you! Why is it so hard to love me back?"

Mason glanced over at Cherise's panic-stricken face. Her life was in danger as long as Lillian had the gun aimed at her, and he knew he had to do something fast. His gun was downstairs on top of the refrigerator, but if he could get to his nightstand, he could get to his other one. In the meantime, he decided to use reverse psychology on her.

"I do love you, Lillian," he answered. "Why do you think I came to D. C.?"

Cherise squinted her eyes at him, not wanting to believe her ears, but then she realized what he was trying to do. He was trying to save her life.

Lillian frowned and said, "I don't believe you."

"You saw me put my suitcase in the car. I was on my way back to you."

Lillian looked into Mason's eyes and searched for the sincerity.

"Where is she going?" Lillian asked, shaking the gun in Cherise's direction.

"We're getting a divorce. She's going to stay with her parents until everything's final."

Lillian thought for a minute. Mason could be telling the truth, but he had said some horrible things to her before he left D.C.

"She'll never leave us alone, Mason. A divorce is not enough. I want her out of our lives forever so we can be together."

Mason took another step toward her and said, "We can be together, but only if you put the gun down. Cherise won't give us any problems."

"How can you be so sure?" she asked.

"I'm sure because she's in love with someone else."

That bit of information got Lillian's attention. Could it be true?

Cherise's body trembled in agony. Tears poured out of her eyes as she listened to Mason's words. He was taking a huge chance, and she wanted to scream out to Lillian that she would never have Mason. She knew, however, that if she proclaimed her feelings for Mason, the crazed woman just might pull the trigger.

"Are you in love with someone else?" Lillian asked Cherise curiously.

As painful as it was to talk about their private life in front of Lillian, she answered, "Yes."

"It doesn't matter," Lillian replied. "You might be in love with someone else now, but there's no guarantee that you won't come back into our lives and give us trouble. Nothing's definite but death."

"Lillian!" Mason yelled to get her attention. "It's over between me and my wife. All we have in common now is the children. I promise. We won't have to worry about her. Let's just go. You don't have to do this. I love you and I love our daughter. I can't wait to meet her."

Tears were now streaming out of Lillian's eyes. Mason discreetly took another step toward Lillian, causing Cherise's eyes to widen. She shook her head and tried to signal him not to approach Lillian. She didn't want him taking any chances, and tried to think of another way to disarm her, but her mind was stricken with fear for her life and the life of her husband.

Vincent drove as fast as he could toward Mason's house. As he drove, he tried calling Mason's cell phone again, but still no answer. He called Cherise's phone and waited. No answer, and there was no answer on the house phone either. The voicemail came on for all three telephones, causing him great concern. Their flight wasn't due to depart for another two and a half hours, so they shouldn't be unreachable over the phone.

"Damn it!" Vincent yelled as he picked up his radio and called dispatch for a black and white to do a drive by his brother's home. He had a bad feeling, and his car couldn't go fast enough for him. He prayed there was a reasonable explanation for their unanswered phones, but something in his gut told him otherwise.

"Don't answer that phone!" Lillian yelled.

Cherise glanced down at her cell phone and said, "It's my lover. If I don't answer, he'll know something's wrong. I'm supposed to meet him, and I'm late."

Lillian walked over to Cherise's cell phone and checked the missed call and saw Vincent's name on the screen.

She aimed the gun at Cherise's head and said, "You think I'm stupid, don't you? You can't play me. That's your goddamn brother-in-law."

"I know," Cherise replied. "He's my lover."

Lillian looked over at Mason and saw the hurt in his eyes.

"She's telling the truth, isn't she?" Lillian asked him.

"I told you she's in love with someone else," he revealed.

Lillian burst out laughing and said, "Wait a minute. You mean to tell me that your wife is giving it up to your brother?"

Mason didn't answer. The muscles in his jaw twitched as Lillian laughed even louder. It hurt, but her laughter was the distraction he needed, so he channeled his pain elsewhere and tried to regroup.

"Don't do this, Lillian. I'll do whatever you want. Just don't hurt my wife."

No!" Cherise yelled.

Lillian smiled and said, "You've been dismissed, bitch," and she pulled the trigger, shooting Cherise.

Mason screamed out Cherise's name in agony as he dove toward Lillian. His actions startled her, causing her to pull the trigger again.

"Mason!" Lillian yelled as she looked down at what she'd done. Blood was starting to seep through his shirt, and he was struggling to breathe.

Sobbing, she tried to help him off the floor. "I'm so sorry, baby. I didn't mean to hurt you. Get up so we can get out of here!"

Mason was becoming weaker by the second, and even though he was shot, his main concern was Cherise. He could see her legs, and she wasn't moving.

Distraught, Lillian continued to apologize to Mason for shooting him. That's when she leaned down, tucked her daughter's picture in his pocket, kissed him on the lips, and shot herself in the head.

Vincent and a patrol officer pulled up at the McKenzie house just as the last shot rang out. He sprinted through the door and up the stairs, where he found Lillian dead and Cherise and Mason severely wounded. He yelled at the police officer accompanying him to call paramedics as he checked Mason and then Cherise. She was hit in the shoulder, but was losing a lot of blood. Mason was more seriously injured, with a gunshot to the chest.

Cherise pulled herself over to her husband and told Vincent to put pressure on his wound. She was in pain and bleeding, but she could see that Mason was in far worse condition.

"Mason, stay with me, baby. You're going to be okay," she encouraged him.

Vincent knelt down next to his brother and said, "Hang in there, bro. Paramedics are on the way."

Tears rolled out of Mason's eyes as he slowly reached up and gripped his brother's hand. Vincent screamed at the officer to rush the paramedics. Cherise's body was shivering, and she felt herself starting to black out. Vincent pulled a blanket off the bed and put it over both of them to keep them from going into shock.

Crying, Cherise kissed Mason's lips and said, "Mason, I love you. You fight, baby. Don't you let her win! Fight!"

He smiled, whispered, "I'm sorry, sweetheart. I love you."

"No, Mason. Fight!" she instructed him again.

Paramedics rushed up the stairs and started administering aid to both Cherise and Mason. Mason looked into his brother's eyes and said, "Take care of my family, bro."

Visibly shaken, Vincent shook his head and said, "You can do that yourself. Just keep breathing, Mason."

Mason closed his eyes, and Cherise screamed out for him, blacking out in the process.

Chapter Nineteen

At the hospital, Vincent waited for word on Cherise and Mason's condition. They were both rushed into surgery as soon as they arrived at the hospital. Vincent gathered his thoughts and placed a call to Jonathan and Patricia, informing them of the shooting. He advised them to bring the children to the hospital, just in case things took a turn for the worse, but he didn't want to think along those lines.

News of the shooting was broadcast as breaking news on all of the local news stations. Information was sketchy, and journalists weren't able to release their names, but they didn't have any problem speculating that the shooting was either related to Mason's former undercover work, or that it was the result of a love triangle. He hated it for the children's sake, but knew there was no way to shelter them from the information. The best thing he could do was tell them as much of the truth as possible.

The hallway was full of police officers, and for safety reasons, Vincent and his family were allowed private access to the waiting room. Patricia prayed, and Jonathan held Janelle in his arms as she quietly sobbed. Mase sat next to his uncle with his head in his hands, obviously hiding his tears. Vincent closed his eyes and prayed a very private prayer in hopes that surgeons would be able to save his brother and Cherise.

Hours passed, and finally a surgeon came in to inform the

family that Cherise was out of surgery and was being moved to the intensive care unit. He told them she was lucky that the bullet missed a vital artery by millimeters. Janelle and Mase begged to see their mother, and the surgeon agreed, but gave them a five-minute time limit.

"What about Mason?" Jonathan asked anxiously. "Is he okay?"

"Unfortunately, the bullet moved though his body, collapsing a lung and lacerating his liver, and like your daughter, he's lost a lot of blood. He's still in surgery, and we're doing everything we can to repair the damage. Mason's strong, but he needs a lot of prayer right now," the surgeon explained. "As soon I know more information, either myself or the surgeon working on him will let you know."

Mase burst into tears upon hearing the information. He'd held back his tears for as long as he could. Vincent hugged him and tried to console him. The waiting was agonizing for all of them. A couple of the detectives on Mason's team brought in coffee for the adults and hot cocoa for the kids, while others officers did what they could to make the family comfortable. Mase and Janelle were anxious to see their parents, but would have to wait a little longer to see their father. In the meantime, Vincent spoke with homicide detectives across the room, to shed as much light on the shooting as possible. He had no idea what transpired leading up to the shooting, but he had a good idea, since Lillian was involved. He was thankful that Cherise was out of surgery, but all of his thoughts now were in the operating room with his brother.

Inside the operating room, surgeons worked frantically to repair the damage to Mason's body. Unbeknownst to the family, he'd coded twice, but they were able to bring him back each time. As he lay there, Mason could hear the beeping sounds of the machines. He felt his body become light, and then heavy, and then light again. He could see the doctors and nurses working on him, but what made him panic the most was when he saw the defibrillator being placed against his heart. The surgeon screamed orders at the nurses as they continued to send the electrical charge to his heart.

"I'm not ready to go!" Mason yelled out, without getting a reaction from the medical staff. "Don't let me die! I have children! They need me!"

He looked around the room and asked, "Where's my wife?"

Still no response. He'd heard about out of body experiences, and the closest he had come to one was when he was taking strong painkillers for his injured spine; but this was different, because he was actually looking at himself and the surgeon operating on him.

"Cherise! Where are you, baby?" he yelled out as he searched the room for his wife. That's when the horrible memory of what happened came back to him. Lillian shot Cherise and then she shot him, but where was she? How could he have brought this woman into their lives? He never dreamed his life could end up where it was now, and he was full of regrets. Mason had expected to be killed on the job, but not by a spurned lover. Now he was faced with the fact that he was either going to have to live with what he'd done, with everyone hating him, or die knowing he'd put the tragic events into motion and ripped his family apart.

The homicide detective pulled his notepad out of his jacket and began to question Vincent.

"Commander, I need you to tell me everything you can about Lillian Green. I know she used to work for the D.A.'s office, but why would she be at your brother's house?"

"Miss Green and my brother worked a lot of cases together. They were friends," Vincent replied, not wanting to reveal the real relationship between Mason and Lillian.

"Commander, I have to be honest with you. This has all the signs of an attempted murder/suicide. If there's anything else you can tell me to shine a light on this, you can help us close this case."

Vincent scratched his head and whispered, "This is a delicate matter, detective, but I'm an officer, so I want this to go away as quietly and quickly as possible. My niece and nephew could lose both of their parents. They're already suffering. I don't want their parents' image dragged through the mud."

"I understand," the detective responded. "Start from the beginning, and I'll do everything I can to keep certain details from being leaked to the media. Agreed?"

"Agreed," Vincent replied as he started telling the detective about Mason's history with Lillian.

Cherise was finally settled in the intensive care unit of the hospital. She was unconscious, but her vital signs looked promising. Janelle and Mase held on to their mother the best they could, avoiding the IVs and the other medical equipment she was hooked up to. Jonathan and Patricia knew they had to hold it together for the children's sake, but they were clearly distraught seeing their only child in the condition she was in. As retired physicians, they understood the severity of her injuries, and while her recovery was promising, they knew that she was at risk of infection, pneumonia, and many other complications.

Vincent finished his interview with the homicide detective and joined his family in Cherise's room. He gave Patricia a loving hug.

"How is she doing?" he asked in a whispering voice.

"The doctors said she's going to be okay," Patricia replied with tears in her eyes. "I never dreamed I would be watching my only child through something like this. I hate seeing my grandchildren go through this too."

Vincent nodded in agreement.

"Listen Patricia, Cherise told me she told you about us. I'm sorry I—"

Patricia held her hand up to Vincent and said, "Not now, Vincent. I don't even want to know. I'm disappointed in all three of you. Right now I want to direct all my energy and prayers to Mason and Cherise. They have these children to live for."

"I hope you can find it in your heart to forgive me," he said, seeking redemption.

She kissed his cheek and said, "Of course I forgive you. Why don't you go check on Mason? We'll stay with Cherise. Once everyone's out of the hospital, we'll all sit down and talk this out as a family. Nobody comes between our family. Never forget that."

Two hours later, Mason came out of surgery on a ventilator in a drug-induced coma. He was in critical condition. Surgeons were able to repair the damage to his lung and liver, but he had a long road ahead of him once he was revived.

Jonathan excused himself from his daughter's room long enough to request that the couple be put together in the intensive care unit. It would make it easier on the children, who needed to be by their parents' side.

The hours seemed to go by quickly as the family continued their vigil over Cherise and Mason. The next evening, Cherise was awake and thankful to be alive, but it broke her heart to see her husband fighting for his life, especially when he began to run a fever.

Later that night, after the children had gone home with Patricia, and Jonathan slept in the recliner, she made her way over to Mason's bed and leaned down close to his ear.

"I know you can hear me, Mason, and I want you to know that I love you and I carry you in my heart. You might not believe that after all we've been through; I still need you."

She reached over and caressed his cheek gently. It hurt her to see Mason in the condition he was in, so she decided to try everything to get him to fight for his life.

"What are you doing out of bed?" Jonathan asked as he joined his daughter at Mason's bedside.

"I needed to talk to him, Daddy. I know he can hear me."

Jonathan helped her back to her bed and said, "I know you did, but next time let me help you. You're still weak, and you could've fallen."

She slid back into her bed and looked back over at Mason. "I'm scared, Daddy. I don't want to lose him."

He covered her with the blanket and said, "Mason's strong. He'll be fine. Just give him some time and pray."

Cherise stared at Mason and thought about their last conversation and the way they looked at each other. They were a team like they were in the beginning of her marriage, and it felt good. Now to have this happen seemed like some type of punishment for the both of them, and it wasn't the type of ending she wanted for her marriage.

Minutes later, the nurse came into the room. She attended to Mason first and then Cherise. She changed out their IV drips, checked Cherise's bandages, injected pain medication into her IV, and made notes on their charts before leaving the room. Cherise's eyes fluttered as the medication took effect quickly, causing her to drift off to sleep.

Jonathan kept a close eye on his daughter and son-in-law. He was anxious to find out how and why this tragedy happened. For now, he would allow his daughter to get well before pressuring her into reliving the shooting.

Jonathan kissed Cherise's forehead and said, "Get some rest, sweetheart. You can talk to Mason more in the morning."

As she slipped into unconsciousness, she mumbled incoherently in her sleep.

The next morning, Vincent and Patricia arrived with the kids. Jonathan seemed irritated the moment Vincent walked into the room.

"Did they have a good night?" he asked.

Jonathan pulled Vincent to the side and said, "I know this might not be the time and place, but what the hell happened to Mason and my daughter?"

Vincent led Jonathan out into the hallway so they could talk privately.

"I'm not sure, but I think Lillian Green tried to kill Cherise, and Mason got shot trying to protect her."

"Who is this Lillian Green woman?" Jonathan asked curiously.

"She was a woman Mason had an affair with a few years ago," he explained reluctantly. "She moved to D.C., but showed up in Atlanta a few weeks ago, telling Mason he was the father of her daughter. He was in the process of trying to get a DNA test when all of this went down."

"Why am I just now hearing about this?" Jonathan asked. "If this woman was dangerous, there should have been precautions taken."

"I agree, but Mason said he had everything under control. He didn't mean for anyone to get hurt, especially C. J. Something went wrong. Have you asked Cherise about it?"

"No, and I don't want to until she's better."

"Since she's awake, the detectives are going to want to talk to her so they can wrap up the case," Vincent explained.

"Not while I'm here," Jonathan answered. "I don't want her going through that until she's ready, and you're able to make it happen, so do it."

Vincent assured Jonathan he would do what he could to hold off the detectives.

Jonathan turned to walk back in the room, but he stopped and turned back to Vincent with a scowl on his face.

"Listen, Vincent, while we're talking, Cherise told us about the two of you. What the hell were you thinking?" he asked. "She is your brother's wife."

"I know who she is, Jonathan, and I don't have to tell you how life was for C. J. and the kids when Mason was working undercover," he answered. "Mason's my brother, and I love him, but I didn't love the person he became back then when he was working the streets. I never meant to have a relationship with C. J. Things just sort of happened. I love her, and I always will."

Jonathan pointed his finger in Vincent's face and said, "That's no excuse. I agree that Mason wasn't the best son-in-law when he was working undercover, but wrong is wrong. You knew better, regardless of how Mason was acting."

"I'm sorry, Jonathan. Patricia has forgiven me, and so has Mason. I can apologize until the day I die, but it doesn't change the way I feel about her."

Jonathan folded his arms and said, "I'm not saying I can't forgive you, son. Cherise is Mason's wife . . . period. Respect it."

Vincent knew he was going to have to eventually answer to the Jernigans about the affair, and Jonathan was wearing him out.

"I'm not trying to beat you up. Cherise told us about Mason and his extramarital affairs. She said they were getting a divorce, but I told her she'd better think about her decision. You young people today take love for granted. I've been married to Patricia for over thirty years, and I never wanted anyone else. Marriage vows are supposed to be sacred and everlasting."

"She's not happy, Jonathan."

"My daughter's happiness means everything to me and her mother. If she was unhappy, she should've talked to Mason and tried to work it out."

"She did try, and Mason made a gallant effort, too, but—"

"But what?" Jonathan asked, interrupting him.

"It's not my place to tell you their business."

Jonathan folded his arms and said, "I don't see why not. You're all up in their business in more ways than one."

Vincent hated that Jonathan saw him as a home wrecker, but it wasn't his place to reveal certain indiscretions. When he remained silent, Jonathan turned to go back into the room and said, "I pray all three of you can live with what you've done to your lives and my grandchildren."

Vincent was left standing in the hallway with his thoughts. Jonathan wasn't pleased with any of their behavior, but in time, Vincent hoped he would come around.

It was at that moment Vincent heard a loud alarm coming from the room. He entered the room and saw Mase was frantically calling out to his father. Nurses and a doctor quickly entered and started working on Mason. He had coded once again. A nurse tried to escort the entire family out of the room so they wouldn't be so traumatized by the medical staff's efforts, but Jonathan and Vincent refused to leave.

"Clear!" the doctor yelled as he placed the defibrillator on Mason's chest and pressed the button.

Vincent looked over at Cherise, who was sobbing hysterically as she called out to Mason.

They worked to revive him for nearly thirty minutes before he was pronounced dead. Vincent fell to his knees where he stood and began to do something he hadn't done since the loss of his parents. He cried openly, and began to mourn the loss of his brother.

Chapter Twenty

Losing Mason was devastating to the entire family, and the children were beyond consoling. The only thing that came close to comforting them was the fact that their mother was now awake. The last forty-eight hours had been challenging, and while Cherise's body was healing, her heart had been shattered. Her children needed her more than ever now, and she was determined to be there for them. She didn't have a full memory of the shooting, but she remembered that Lillian was involved, and it caused her distress and nausea. She wanted to get out of the hospital so she could hold her children and grieve for Mason.

Two days later and against the doctor's wishes, Cherise left the hospital. The only thing that allowed the doctors to feel comfortable releasing her was the fact that she was being sent home in the care of both of her parents, who were retired physicians. Jonathan helped Cherise into the wheelchair, while Mase carried her garment bag. Janelle held her mother's hand and asked, "Does your shoulder hurt, Momma?"

She touched her daughter's face lovingly and said, "Just a little bit, sweetheart, but I'm okay."

Patricia got final instructions from Cherise's doctor. She assured him that Cherise was in good hands, and if anything changed, they would bring her back to the hospital immediately.

Vincent had spent the last twenty-four hours trying to make funeral arrangements for Mason. It was heart wrenching, but it had to be done. There were some parts of the arrangements that were textbook, since he was a police officer, but he wanted to get Cherise's approval for the bulk of the funeral before finalizing the plans.

He stepped out of the funeral home and looked up at the sky. It was cloudy, with the threat of severe thunderstorms, a true barometer of his feelings.

Since the shooting, Vincent and Jonathan were the only people who had set foot in the McKenzie home. They needed to retrieve clothing and other belongings for the children and Cherise. They also hired an agency to rid the bedroom of any evidence of the shooting before putting the house on the market. While there were some great memories in the home, the shooting was overshadowing everything good that had taken place there. There was no way on earth Cherise could ever lay eyes on the room where Mason was tragically taken from her.

At the Jernigans' house, Cherise was settled into her room. The pain medication had worn off, and pain was coming back with a vengeance. Patricia administered more pain medication to her just as Vincent arrived at the house. Jonathan welcomed him before joining the children in the family room.

"How's C. J.?" he asked as he hugged his niece and nephew.

Jonathan picked up the newspaper and answered, "In pain. Patricia's upstairs with her now."

Vincent headed toward the stairs, meeting Patricia in the hallway.

"Hello, Vincent."

"Hello, Patricia."

She cupped his face and asked, "How are you holding up? You look exhausted. Have you eaten?"

He hugged her and said, "I'm as well as to be expected. I can't eat or sleep. I still can't accept that he's gone."

"I'm praying for you, Vincent. We have a kitchen full of food that people have brought by. You need to put something in your stomach and then try to get some sleep," she responded as she walked toward the kitchen.

"Is C. J. asleep?"

"I just gave her some pain medication. You're welcome to go see her."

Vincent climbed the stairs and slowly opened the door to her bedroom. He walked over to the bed and looked down at her angelic face. Tears stained her face and pillow as she slept, and it caused a huge lump in his throat. Not wanting to disturb her, he turned to leave the room, but her soft voice called out to him.

"How long have you been here?" she asked.

He slowly walked over to the bed and sat down in the chair. "Not long," he replied as he took her hand into his. "How are you feeling?"

"Terrible," she answered. "How are the arrangements coming along?"

"I have it ready for you to look over when you feel up to it," he said as he stroked her hand in a soothing manner.

"I let him down, didn't I?" she asked.

"No, I'm the one who let him down. I should've been there. There's no way that woman should've gotten to you guys."

Sadness overtook her even more as they continued to talk.

"She would've shot you too if you had been there."

Vincent's jaw twitched as he tried to stifle his tears.

"This family has too many lies and secrets," she said as her eyes fluttered. The medication was starting to take effect, making her extremely sleepy.

"What are you talking about, C. J?" he asked.

"You know I love you, and would never intentionally hurt you, right?" she asked breathlessly.

"Of course I do. What is it?"

Her heart was pounding so loudly that she felt like it was echoing in the room and about to burst out of her chest.

"God, you're going to kill me," she stated as she broke out in a cold sweat.

Her nervousness was now making him nervous. "What is it, C. J?"

With shallow breath, she said, "Mason was not a perfect man, but he was a good man. In spite of the drama he put me through, he was a great father to our children. I love him, and I'll always love him, but you also deserve to know the truth."

Her speech was slurring, and as she spoke, her eyes closed, but she had his attention. He wanted to know what she was trying to say.

"The truth about what?" he asked curiously.

"Mason wasn't Janelle's biological father."

That's when Vincent's heart nearly stopped beating. His body tensed and he started to tremble. "What?"

Before falling into a deep sleep, she mumbled, "Janelle isn't Mason's daughter. She's yours."

Cherise had just laid some mind-boggling news on him. Could it be true, or was it the medication making her delirious? He needed answers, and he needed them now.

"C. J.? Wake up!" he called out to her, but she was out, and he would have to wait until later to verify what she'd told him. He planned to be sitting right there when she woke up.

In the meantime, how could he look into Janelle's eyes and be cool? He'd always suspected she was his daughter, but he'd seen the DNA test with his own eyes, and he wasn't a match.

Patricia stuck her head inside the bedroom door and said, "Vincent, there's food downstairs. You need to come eat, and I'm not taking no for an answer."

"I'm not hungry, Patricia," he replied as he stared into Cherise's face.

Patricia walked over to him and grabbed his hand. "Cherise is going to be asleep for at least three hours. She's not going anywhere."

Reluctantly, he left the room, but vowed to return to get more information out of Cherise as soon as she woke up.

After nibbling on some food, Vincent spent some time with the children and greeted some officers as they came by the house to pay their respects. It was nearly eight o'clock before Cherise woke up again, and when she did, Vincent was sitting in the recliner next to her bed. Patricia prepared her a plate of mashed potatoes and gravy and a little baked chicken; however, she was unable to eat more than a few spoonfuls. Once Patricia left the room, Vincent immediately started questioning her about Janelle.

"The lab made a mistake," she revealed. "A week or so after the first DNA results came back, I got another package with the correct results and a letter apologizing for the mix-up."

Vincent paced the floor, clearly distraught by the news. He couldn't believe what he was hearing. "Where is it? I want to see it."

"I burned it, Vincent," she admitted. "I never planned on telling anybody about it. Mason and I started working on our marriage, so I decided it was going to be too much for us to handle. I just wanted it to go away."

"That was selfish. What about me?" he asked. "Don't you think I deserved to know the truth, even if you didn't tell Mason?"

"I'm sorry."

He stared into her eyes and then asked, "Is that supposed to comfort me?"

"Under the circumstances, yes, it should."

They sat in silence for nearly five minutes, but it seemed like hours. Vincent was still trying to absorb the one bright light in the darkness surrounding the past few days, and Cherise was trying to cope with her loss and finalizing Mason's services.

"How's your arm?" Vincent asked to change the subject.

She touched the bandaged area and said, "I'll be okay. Where's the paperwork you need me to look at?"

He walked over to the dresser and pulled some papers out of a large envelope. He handed them to her and said, "If you don't feel up to it, you can wait until morning."

Tears dropped out of eyes as she held out her hand. "Why put off the inevitable? This has to be done whether I do it now or later."

"Do you want some privacy?" he asked as he picked up a box of tissue and held it out to her.

"Just give me a minute," she requested as she stared down at the rough draft of the obituary. The picture Vincent chose was one of Mason in uniform. He was so handsome, and his eyes were full of life.

"I've always loved this picture."

"The kids helped," he revealed. "Mase found a poem from him and Janelle that I put on the second page."

As Cherise read the poems, her eyes were clouded with even more tears. "They're beautiful. Mase did a good job."

"Are you in agreement with the order of services?" he asked.

"I don't want it to be extremely long. It's going to be hard enough as it is on the children."

She scanned the rest of the program and made some minor changes to the order of service, and added a tribute page. A couple of hours later, the program and arrangements were finalized, and the date was set for two days later.

Mason's funeral was a massive, joyous celebration of life. Hundreds of officers from all over the country were there in uniform to pay their respects to their fallen brother. Cherise was still in pain, but it was nothing compared to the pain in her heart. She had to be strong for the children. They were her priority.

She was beautiful, dressed in her black belted dress, trimmed in white. She was a vision of poise and loveliness as she walked into the tabernacle on her son's arm. Vincent, Jonathan, and Patricia followed with Janelle, as a host of other relatives, cousins, and close friends filled up the pews. The service was lively and jubilant. Cherise didn't want it to be depressing. Mason had touched an abundance of lives and brought joy to a lot of people, herself included, and she wanted him to be celebrated.

After the burial, Mase escorted his mother back to the limo. Before she could get inside the car, she was approached by a woman and a child.

"Excuse me, Mrs. McKenzie, but do you have a moment?"

Cherise studied the woman and asked, "How can I help you?"

Vincent walked over to Cherise and asked, "Is there a problem?"

The lady waved him off and said, "Oh, no. I was just asking Mrs. McKenzie if she had a moment. I need to talk to her."

"About what?" Vincent asked with a frown on his face.

Janelle walked over to her mother, wrapped her arms around her waist, and asked, "Who are you?"

"Sweetheart, you and Mase go ahead and get in the car. I need to talk to this nice lady for a second."

Once Janelle and Mase were isolated in the car, the lady said, "I'm not here to cause you any more pain. I can see that your husband was a loved man. I'm deeply sorry for your loss and the pain you're going through," she announced.

"Thank you."

The lady put her arms around the little girl's shoulders and said, "I wish I was doing this under better circumstances, but there is no other way to tell you."

"Tell me what?" Cherise asked.

"This is my granddaughter. Her name is McKenzie, and Mason is her father. Lillian Green was my daughter, and I'm so sorry for what she did to you and your family."

Cherise immediately got lightheaded upon hearing the news. She stared in the little girl's eyes and saw Mason's face.

Vincent looked at the little girl and saw the same thing. He was stunned at how much she looked like Mase. She was definitely a McKenzie, and no DNA test could tell them what they saw with their own eyes.

"Mrs. Green, I'm Mason's brother. We spoke over the telephone. I appreciate the information you gave me about Lillian. I just hate I was unable to stop her before she ripped my family apart."

She held her hand out to Vincent and said, "So am I. I wish you had found me sooner. It's nice to meet you."

"Vincent, can you give us some privacy?" Cherise asked. "Also tell the limo driver to go ahead and take the kids home with Momma and Daddy. We can go in the second limo."

Vincent did as he was instructed, and then mingled with several officers in order to give Cherise the privacy she requested.

"What can I do for you, Mrs. Green?"

She looked down at her granddaughter with tears in her eyes and said, "I'm dying. I have cancer, and doctors are giving me less than a year to live. With my daughter gone, I'm the only family McKenzie has left. I know it's asking a lot of you under the circumstances, but I need someone to raise her for me. I can't let her go into foster care."

Cherise put her hand up to Mrs. Green, interrupting her. "How dare you come here and ask me something like that? Have you no respect for me and my children?"

"I know it seems completely far fetched, but I knew Mason well. I don't mean this with any disrespect, but there was a time that he loved my daughter. They were happy. I didn't know he was married."

Cherise walked toward the other limo and said, "I'm leaving."

Mrs. Green reached out for Cherise's hand and said, "Mrs. McKenzie, please. Lillian had her issues and was struggling with a mental disorder. The woman that shot you and your husband was not my daughter. That's why I was raising McKenzie in Kentucky."

"I'm sorry about your circumstances, but I can't help you."

"I'm going to be starting chemo soon. All I'm asking of you is to think about it. I can't go to my grave knowing my granddaughter is in foster care."

Mrs. Green reached inside her purse and gave Cherise her address and telephone number. "I hope and pray that I hear from you soon."

And just like that, they were gone. Vincent, who was watching from afar, walked over to Cherise and asked, "What did she want?"

She tucked the small piece of paper inside her purse and said, "She dying, and she asked me to raise Mason's daughter."

If she thought she was hurting before, it was nothing compared to the excruciating pain she was in now.

"What are you going to do?" Vincent asked as he opened the car door for Cherise.

She looked at Vincent and asked, "How can I raise that child? I feel sorry for them, but I can't do it. Every time I look at her, it'll be a reminder of what happened. She's your niece. Why don't you raise her?"

Vincent was silent for a moment, and then he asked, "What would Mason want you to do?"

Cherise pulled a tissue out of her purse and wiped the tears running down her face.

Epilogue

Three weeks had passed since Mason's untimely death. Cherise was in physical therapy, and she had their belongings put in storage until they found another home. In the meantime, they were living with her parents, and the children were slowly getting back into a routine. There were good days and bad days, and everyone was still trying to come to terms with the fact that Mason was gone. Cherise had a lot of legal matters to take care of, one of which included the reading of Mason's will. They had made out wills together, but Cherise was stunned to find out that Mason had revised his in recent weeks. He had left her a very apologetic and tender letter regarding his mistakes over the past few years. As she read the letter, she knew without a doubt that Mason loved her and had truly forgiven her for her affair with Vincent.

As the attorney read the will to her, she was expecting to find out that Mason had done a complete revision; however, the only thing he had changed was where he named his children. Originally, he had provisions set up for Janelle and Mason Jr. by name; however, he revised it to say *his surviving children*, which would now include his daughter, McKenzie. Cherise wasn't concerned with the money, and was very capable of taking care of her children financially. They'd always planned for money to be put into a trust for their children if anything happened to them, leaving a clause for the disbursement of funds for the daily care of their children. They'd done well with investments and savings, and financially, they were secure.

Cherise left the attorney's office with a lot on her mind. As she sat in her car, she pulled Mrs. Green's number out of her purse and stared at it for several minutes. Then she tried to put herself in her shoes, and asked herself, what would she do in that situation? Her cell phone interrupted her thoughts, and she put the paper back inside her purse.

"Hello?"

"Are you okay?" Vincent asked. "Lorenzo called me, and was concerned about you. How did the reading go?"

"I think Mason was convinced that the little girl was his daughter. He changed his will."

Vincent was surprised by Mason's actions, but agreed with Cherise that his brother may have done some soul searching and come to some type of conclusion regarding the little girl.

"I support you in whatever you decide," Vincent answered. "What Mrs. Green is asking you is serious, and something you can't take lightly."

Cherise started the car and said, "I know. I have to go. I'll call you later."

Later would be twenty-four hours later. When Cherise left downtown, she drove straight to the Hartsfield-Jackson Airport and boarded a plane to Louisville, Kentucky. She felt like she needed some type of resolution to her marriage that would allow her to feel good about the mistakes she had made. On the plane ride there, she kept hearing her voice say over and over in her head, *what would you do?* It was haunting, but it was also liberating for her soul. She was still a little apprehensive about making such a life-altering decision without talking to her family first, but she was acting on instinct, and every fiber in her body was telling her she was doing the right thing. She would have a very mature conversation with her children over the telephone tonight in her hotel room before returning to Atlanta, and then they would talk some more once she returned home.

The next morning, Cherise returned to Atlanta accompanied by Jillian McKenzie Green, a bright-eyed, inquisitive preteen. On the plane, Cherise could tell the girl was a little nervous about living with her, but after a long conversation with her, along with her grandmother, she was anxious to meet her new family. Cherise assured Mrs. Green that she would bring McKenzie back for visits and let her know that she would do right by her husband's wishes.

When Cherise pulled up in front of her parents' home, Janelle and Mase ran out and met the car in the driveway.

Janelle opened the car door and asked, "Are you really my sister?"

McKenzie nodded as Janelle took her by the hand and led her up on the porch.

"Mom, are you sure about this?" Mase asked.

She hugged her son and said, "More than ever, but are you sure you can handle it?"

He kissed her cheek and said, "She's my sister, right?"

"Right," she replied then asked him to get McKenzie's suitcase out of the trunk.

Eight months later, McKenzie's grandmother succumbed to cancer and died in her sleep.

Cherise had scaled back her responsibilities in the CSI office after Mason's death, and only worked in the lab. She needed stable hours for the children, and after a lot of searching, they found a suitable home closer to her parents, where they could start rebuilding their lives with happy memories.

McKenzie seemed to be settled in with her new family, but Vincent was still trying to come to terms with the loss of his brother and the fact that Janelle was his daughter. He felt lost, incomplete, and needed some type of stability in his life. It didn't help that he was still very much in love with Cherise. They'd kept their relationship strictly as in-laws, but he wasn't able to hold back his feelings anymore, so he invited her over for dinner one night and took a chance on asking her to marry him.

When he presented her with the ring, she pushed it away.

"I can't marry you, Vincent."

"Why not? You've stepped out on faith with everything except us."

She stood and walked out on the balcony and let the cool breeze blow over her body.

He joined her out on the balcony and asked, "What are you afraid of?"

"Aren't you concerned about what people will think?"

"I don't give a damn about what people think," he replied angrily.

"If I say yes, then what?" she asked. "Are you going to want to tell Janelle you're her father?"

"I thought about it and decided that if we felt like she needed to know, it would be best if we waited until she was old enough to handle it. They've been through a lot. You've been through a lot."

She reached over and took his hand into hers and said, "I appreciate that."

He took her left hand into his and slid the ring on her finger and asked, "Are you ready to step out on faith?"

Cherise hugged him lovingly and said, "Only if there will be no more unspoken lies."

He kissed her and said, "I think I can do that. What about you?"

"Consider it done. And on that note, yes, Vincent, I'll marry you."

ORDER FORM
URBAN BOOKS, LLC
78 E. Industry Ct
Deer Park, NY 11729

Name: (please print):_____

Address: _____

City/State: _____

Zip: _____

QTY	TITLES	PRICE
	16 ½ On The Block	$14.95
	16 On The Block	$14.95
	Betrayal	$14.95
	Both Sides Of The Fence	$14.95
	Cheesecake And Teardrops	$14.95
	Denim Diaries	$14.95
	Happily Ever Now	$14.95
	Hell Has No Fury	$14.95
	If It Isn't love	$14.95
	Last Breath	$14.95
	Loving Dasia	$14.95
	Say It Ain't So	$14.95

Shipping and Handling - add $3.50 for 1st book then $1.75 for each additional book.

Please send a check payable to:

Urban Books, LLC

Please allow 4 - 6 weeks for delivery

ORDER FORM
URBAN BOOKS, LLC
78 E. Industry Ct
Deer Park, NY 11729

Name: (please print):_____

Address: _____

City/State: _____

Zip: _____

QTY	TITLES	PRICE
	The Cartel	$14.95
	The Cartel#2	$14.95
	The Dopeman's Wife	$14.95
	The Prada Plan	$14.95
	Gunz And Roses	$14.95
	Snow White	$14.95
	A Pimp's Life	$14.95
	Hush	$14.95
	Little Black Girl Lost 1	$14.95
	Little Black Girl Lost 2	$14.95
	Little Black Girl Lost 3	$14.95
	Little Black Girl Lost 4	$14.95

Shipping and Handling - add $3.50 for 1st book then $1.75 for each additional book.
Please send a check payable to:
Urban Books, LLC
Please allow 4 - 6 weeks for delivery

ORDER FORM
URBAN BOOKS, LLC
78 E. Industry Ct
Deer Park, NY 11729

Name: (please print):_____

Address: _____

City/State: _____

Zip: _____

QTY	TITLE	
	A Man's Worth	$14.95
	Abundant Rain	$14.95
	Battle Of Jericho	$14.95
	By The Grace Of God	$14.95
	Dance Into Destiny	$14.95
	Divorcing The Devil	
	Forsaken	
	Grace And Mercy	$14.95
	Guilty & Not Guilty Of Love	$14.95
	His Woman, His Wife His Widow	$14.95
	Illusion	$14.95
	The LoveChild	$14.95

Shipping and Handling - add $3.50 for 1st book then $1.75 for each additional book.

Please send a check payable to:

Urban Books, LLC

Please allow 4 - 6 weeks for delivery